Skye stared at Benoit, waiting for him to laugh and tell her it was all a joke.

"You can't be serious" were the only words to escape her lips.

"I am," he said, his blue eyes hardening like icicles. "I have something you want—" the dismissive shrug of his shoulders just plain irritated her "—and you could be something I need. It's a simple exchange."

"Exchange? It's not an exchange. It's a *marriage*," she couldn't help but cry, her mind scrambling to process what was happening, and racing as he offered the one thing she needed and then pulled it from her reach. "You're barbaric."

"No, barbaric would be kidnapping you and forcing you to marry me. But I'm not. I'm offering you a deal—"

"A deal?" she demanded, horrified at how quickly Benoit had turned from someone sharing confidences to contracts.

"You don't have to take it."

"But we need the map," she insisted.

"And I need a wife," he said determinedly.

The Diamond Inheritance

A map that leads...to forever?

When Skye, Star and Summer find out their mother is gravely ill, they know they have to act— quick! Yet the announcement at their estranged grandfather's funeral of a windfall for the Soames sisters could be the answer to all their prayers. Only, to secure the fortune, they *must* track down the Soames family diamonds. And their unexpected treasure trail will bring each of them into close quarters with a dangerously irresistible billionaire...

Grab your passport and escape with...

Benoit and Skye's story

Terms of Their Costa Rican Temptation

Available now!

And look out for Star's and Summer's stories

Coming soon!

Pippa Roscoe

TERMS OF THEIR COSTA RICAN TEMPTATION

HARLEQUIN
PRESENTS

HARLEQUIN®
PRESENTS®

Recycling programs
for this product may
not exist in your area.

ISBN-13: 978-1-335-40349-0

Terms of Their Costa Rican Temptation

Copyright © 2021 by Pippa Roscoe

This edition published by arrangement with Harlequin Books S.A.

For questions and comments about the quality of this book,
please contact us at CustomerService@Harlequin.com.

Harlequin Enterprises ULC
22 Adelaide St. West, 40th Floor
Toronto, Ontario M5H 4E3, Canada
www.Harlequin.com

Printed in U.S.A.

Pippa Roscoe lives in Norfolk near her family and makes daily promises to herself that this is the day she'll leave the computer to take a long walk in the countryside. She can't remember a time when she wasn't dreaming about handsome heroes and innocent heroines. Totally her mother's fault, of course—she gave Pippa her first romance to read at the age of seven! She is inconceivably happy that she gets to share those daydreams with you all. Follow her on Twitter, @pipparoscoe.

Books by Pippa Roscoe

Harlequin Presents

Virgin Princess's Marriage Debt
Demanding His Billion-Dollar Heir
Rumors Behind the Greek's Wedding
Playing the Billionaire's Game

Once Upon a Temptation

Taming the Big Bad Billionaire

The Winners' Circle

A Ring to Take His Revenge
Claimed for the Greek's Child
Reclaimed by the Powerful Sheikh

Visit the Author Profile page
at Harlequin.com for more titles.

For Rani.

Because sometimes all you need is friendship and laughter to put the world right again.

Xx

PROLOGUE

SKYE SOAMES TOOK a deep breath that quivered at the back of her throat for a moment before she drew it into her lungs, hoping that her sisters hadn't noticed. Not for the first time she wondered what the three of them were doing in Norfolk on an unseasonably cold, grey miserable day, standing beside the coffin of a man they had never met.

She clenched her jaw against the cutting wind as it hit her like a slap. They'd been picked up from their small home on the outskirts of the New Forest by a limousine—neighbours frowning and whispering into their hands as they peered through white lace curtains, as if they hadn't had a lifetime of gossip already. But four hours in a car that glided over concrete had cocooned her and her sisters in a warm, contented state of confusion until they had caught sight of the stone church and the Gothic graveyard beside it.

They were here to...what? Pay their respects?

To a man who had kicked out his only daughter at the age of seventeen and cut her off without a penny or word ever since? Because until today that was all they had ever known about their grandfather, Elias Soames.

Summer, her youngest sister, shifted on her feet and drew her dark wool coat around her middle, her face strangely pale against the blonde hair she'd pulled back into a messy ponytail. So very different from Skye's own brown hair, carefully wrapped into a neat bun, and just as different from the long vibrant, fiery red strands the wind whipped across Star's cheeks. A difference that came from each sister's father. Some might have called them half-sisters, but to Skye, Summer and Star there was nothing half about the bond between them. Star's hand came up to brush her Titian hair back, revealing startling green eyes sparkling with a sheen that looked suspiciously like tears.

'Star?'

'It's just so sad,' she said.

'We never met him. He abandoned our—'

'Ashes to ashes, dust to dust…' The words spoken by the priest cut through Summer's response as if in admonishment and another blast of icy-cold air trickled down Skye's spine. She shivered, not for the grandfather she had never known, but for another funeral, one yet to come. One that threatened to rock the very foundations of Skye and her sisters' lives.

Mariam Soames hadn't been able to attend the funeral because of her treatment schedule—if you could call sipping on herbal teas and CBD tablets treatment. Thanks to the postcode lottery that determined access to specific treatments on the NHS, they'd lost out. Big time. And it had only encouraged their alternative lifestyle living mother further into 'natural treatments'.

Skye had spent more midnight hours than she could count trying to work out how to fund the life-saving health care privately, or even a very costly move into another area where Mariam stood a better chance of treatment. But the housing costs in the nearest health region where that might happen were four times more expensive than what they paid now and, no matter the calculations, they just couldn't make it work. Besides, Mariam didn't want to move, she was focused on quality of life not quantity. Skye's heart twisted that she couldn't find a way to achieve both for her mother.

She looked up at the large house in the distance. Her mother had insisted that even had she been well enough she wouldn't have come. Mariam Soames had said all she needed to her father the night she had left Norfolk thirty-seven years ago.

Elias's lawyer nodded, announcing the end of the small service that marked the end of a man's life. No one else had been in attendance. Clearly Elias Soames had not been a popular figure in the community, leaving the mourners to number five, including the priest.

The lawyer walked them back to the limousine and chose to sit up front with the driver, effectively preventing any conversation until they reached the estate. Skye felt sick at the thought of her grandfather having enough money to fund his daughter's treatment and then some, and felt shame knowing her primary motivation for being here—the will.

Barely five minutes later the car pulled into a grand sweeping drive that took them towards their grandfather's home and Skye's jaw wasn't the only one in the car to drop.

It might not have had the grandeur of the estate from *Downton Abbey*—Summer's favourite TV show—but it wasn't far off. The sprawling ancient building revealed itself in glimpses as the car took the large twists and turns of the drive towards an impressive set of steps at the main entrance, which finally revealed the house in its entirety.

'Holy—' Star's curse was cut short by a not-so-gentle shoulder-shove from Skye, who had no wish to incur any further disdain from Elias's lawyer, Mr Beamish. But it had managed to draw a spark of something to Summer's grey eyes—a spark that had been absent for the last few weeks.

Skye stepped out of the car and was forced to crane her neck to look up at the glorious building. This was…unimaginable. Her mother had walked away from this? There had to be…

'There are over twenty rooms in the main section of the house, but though the east and west wings have been closed off for quite some time now, they also boast a modest fifteen apiece. I'm afraid we have to hurry things along a bit,' he claimed, barely stopping for breath. 'You'll understand why shortly. Follow me.'

With that, he turned on his heel and disappeared into the bowels of the house. Skye and her sisters followed him down dark hallways with moth-eaten carpets, various pieces of antique furniture, sideboards on which sat china bowls of scentless aged potpourri and walls covered in old dusty paintings of ancestors Skye couldn't even begin to imagine. She saw her sisters' heads sweeping from side to side as if to take it all in. But Skye focused only on Mr Beamish as he led them into what was clearly the estate office. One of them had to keep their head on straight and focus on the situation. And, as always, it would be her.

He gestured for them to sit in the three chairs

provided, facing the beautiful and clearly ancient wooden desk. Only when they had done so did Mr Beamish take his place opposite them. Skye watched as he pulled a raft of papers from his briefcase and began the formalities of the reading of the will. Whether it was exhaustion from the day's early start or the particular pitch of his monotone voice, she couldn't keep his words in her head for long and her mind wandered as freely as her eyes around the room. They caught on a large oil painting just behind Mr Beamish.

The image was quite startling, and she knew without a shadow of a doubt that she was staring at a portrait of her grandfather. He looked…mean. And miserable. And nothing like his daughter, who had more laughter, more love in her than she could contain, both traits often trailing in her wake. Skye's mother might be flighty, might have little to no thought of practicalities and necessities, but she loved greatly.

So different from the malicious intent in the eyes of Elias Soames looming up behind Mr Beamish as he delivered his last will and testament. And then her mind snagged on what the lawyer had just said.

'I'm sorry…what?' she asked. Shock cut through her, as if her body had reacted before comprehending what the words had meant.

'As I said, Ms Soames. The entire estate will be

yours, on certain conditions. For five generations the entail known as the Soames diamonds have been missing. Much like his father, and his father's father before him and so on, Elias had been desperately trying to recover them. The specifics of his search are in this folder here,' he said, pushing the folder only halfway towards the women. 'Before his death, my client made the stipulation that you will inherit the entire estate—to do with as you will—on the condition that you are able to retrieve the Soames diamonds within two months of his death.'

Skye was speechless, her mind hurtling at the speed of light through the possibilities this might mean. For them. For their mother.

'So we could sell the estate?' Star demanded.

Mr Beamish nodded. 'If you find the diamonds, yes.'

'Is this even legal?' Skye asked, even while her mind screamed, *I don't care!*

Mr Beamish had the grace to look embarrassed, but not to answer the question. 'Should you fail to discover their whereabouts, then the estate and the entire entail will revert to the National Trust. I believe the deadline set by the will fails to allow for enough time to contest the will. Furthermore, a legal battle would be costly and time-consuming and the two-month deadline is immovable.'

'But—'

Mr Beamish cleared his throat over Summer's protest and pushed on. 'A provision has been set aside for any expenses needed for your endeavours—expenses that I will be able to approve and release as requested. The last stipulation is that one of you must remain in residence at the estate for the entire two months.'

Mr Beamish sucked in a discreet lungful of air as if he'd had to force the words out in one go, no matter how distasteful he had found them.

'You can, of course, choose to refuse the terms, upon which the entire estate and entail will revert immediately to the National Trust. It is clearly a lot to think on. Rooms have been made available for your use this evening, and we will meet again in the morning to hear your final decision.'

With another firm nod, the man left with barely a goodbye—running for the hills, Skye thought. The room was silent until a gasp of horrified laughter erupted from Summer.

'Missing diamonds! How romantic,' Star said on a dramatic sigh.

'That's what you took from all this?' Skye demanded of her whimsical middle sister. 'Romance?'

'Yes! It's *so* romantic,' she insisted, even as Skye shook her head.

Summer had already pulled the thick file which

promised to contain details of Elias's attempts to uncover the location of the Soames diamonds towards her from across the table.

'I can't take two months off. I have a job,' Skye insisted, already torn between practicalities and the possibility of what the terms of the will meant.

'A job from which you've never taken a holiday,' Summer said absently, already scanning through the pages of the file. 'Rob would give you anything you asked, and you know it. You just don't ask.'

'Well, it's not long until school's out for the summer,' Star pressed on, covering the need for Skye to respond to Summer's unusually blunt observation. 'I'm sure they'll let me take the rest of the term off. And Summer's just finished her degree so… Oh, this could be so much fun.'

Fun wasn't what Skye was thinking. She was thinking that if they did manage to find the missing jewels, then perhaps they'd be able to cover their mother's medical bills. Pay for even better treatment. And perhaps… But she stopped her mind from going there. Skye had never put much faith in wishes and prayers like Star had.

'If we found them, we could sell the estate…' Summer said. 'Or at least mortgage it?'

'A mortgage we'd never be able to pay back,' replied Skye.

'But how are we supposed to find jewels that have been missing since…?' Star said, ignoring the practicalities as usual.

'1871,' Summer said, glancing up from the folder for the first time.

'And, even if we did, how *would* we sell it?' Skye asked.

Summer looked away, as if considering. 'I might…know someone,' she said with a shrug of her shoulder.

'You might know someone who happens to have…what? Several hundred million in the bank to buy all this?' The look in her sister's eyes made Skye feel bad about her apparent scepticism. 'Summer—'

'I do,' she replied, ignoring the bite of Skye's words. 'It's a long shot, but yeah. And besides, we don't need several hundred million. We just need enough.'

Skye nodded in return. Just enough to cover Mariam's medical bills.

'Oohh, I love an adventure.'

Skye and Summer shared an eye roll over their sister's excitement.

'So, we're actually doing this?' Skye asked, tempering the unwanted excitement beginning to build in her stomach. She might have spent her life grounding her siblings to counter the airy dreams of their mother, but even she couldn't deny that there was something thrilling about the idea of going on an actual treasure hunt. It was a silly feeling, something that was almost naughty, as if it were a guilty pleasure her heart just couldn't deny as it thrummed quickly in her body.

When Summer and Star nodded, sharing looks of excitement and hope, just for once Skye allowed herself to imagine that this could be the start of a thrilling adventure.

CHAPTER ONE

TWO WEEKS LATER, Skye was finishing up her final search of the last room in the west wing and decided, pulling cobwebs from her hair, that there was nothing thrilling about fruitlessly searching through decades of dust. Beamish hadn't been lying when he said the two wings had been closed for years.

By the time she pushed open the door to the library that had become the Soames sisters' base of operations, she found Star hauling a portrait that must have been nearly one hundred and fifty years old across the room.

'Should you be doing that?' Skye queried.

'Why not?' Tug. 'I thought—' tug '—that it would be good inspiration,' tug.

'Because it might be worth a fair bit of money?' Summer replied without looking up from the mounds of paper she had spread out on the table in front of her. Skye winced at the sound of the gilt frame scraping against the wooden floor as

Star shoved it up against one of the many book-cases in the room.

'There. The last time the diamonds were seen. Catherine Soames' wedding portrait.'

All three of the girls repressed a shiver at the thought of their great-great-grandmother being forced to marry her cousin. Elias's research had been surprisingly detailed. Then again, four generations of Soames men had been looking for the diamonds ever since they'd gone missing from Duke Anthony Soames's private chambers two nights after the painting had been finished.

'Well, they weren't in the west wing, just like they weren't in the east wing,' Skye said, filling them in on the results of her searches. 'Though, from the damage I've seen, I think Elias thought they were hidden in the walls because there are huge holes knocked into them, dust and plaster and God knows what else all over the place. Honestly, it looks as if Elias went at them with a sledgehammer.'

'Perhaps he was mad and that's why Mum didn't want to talk about him?' Star wondered out loud.

'Perhaps it ran in the family. According to the notes here, after Anthony had his valet arrested and imprisoned for the theft, he then decided that Catherine had hidden them, even if he couldn't prove it, or even understand how she might have done it,' Summer said, looking up from the file that seemed to be permanently glued to her hands.

'I hope she *did* hide them. He sounds like a miserable creature.' Smiling at Star's unique description, Skye flipped on the light switch. Although the library was a great place for them to gather, she didn't like how dark it always was.

Sinking down into one of the leather armchairs, she struggled to remain optimistic. Taking up the terms of the will had given them purpose, a goal, something to work towards for their mother. But two weeks in and it was beginning to seem hopeless. Not that she'd ever say as much to Star and Summer. They relied on her, they needed her to be the one to spur them on.

'I think we should move to another room,' Star said, the floaty material of her wide-armed shirt hanging low as she reached out to touch the old leather spines of the books. 'It makes me feel… hinky.'

'Hinky?' Summer asked with a laugh.

'Yeah…just wonky, somehow.'

Skye frowned. She'd never really noticed it before but, now that Star had said it, she knew what her sister meant. Skye tried to look at the room with fresh eyes, rather than ones that had seen it for more hours than she would have wished. The little library, the women's library, Catherine's library. The room had more names for it than any other in the entire estate and, even though it paled in comparison to the Duke's library, all of the sisters had preferred it here, despite the darkness which, now Skye was looking at it, must have had something to do with the—

'The windows!' Summer exclaimed, at the exact moment Skye had realised the same thing. 'The shelves on the left-hand side... I think...' Her words were cut off as Star ran out of the room into the hallway, peering back into the library, then disappearing off to the next room along and reappearing again.

'The room—it's smaller than it should be!' Star practically screamed and Skye tried to suppress uncharitable frustration at the sister who had most definitely taken after their mother in her sense of both romance and adventure. Skye felt a painfully familiar sense of longing that she was ashamed of. A longing to be more like them, a longing to join in with the fun. But then she would be even less like her father, whose serious, quiet, non-confrontational nature was so very different to Mariam. And she clung to whatever she could of her father because when he'd remarried he'd just seemed to get further and further away from her.

Pushing aside the stab of pain brought by her train of thought, Skye focused on what Summer was doing—pulling out some of the ancient tomes lining the left-hand shelves and piling them up on the floor.

'Skye, can you—'

'Coming,' she said, leaning into the thrill of possibly finding the jewels as a distraction.

'Star, these books are hundreds of years old, please don't just—'

The thwack of another large tome hitting the floor made Summer wince.

'Sorry, it's just so…'

'Exciting, yeah we get it,' Skye mumbled under her breath. Surely if this was the final resting place of the jewels someone would have found them by now?

Two shelves cleared, Summer was running her hand underneath the wooden shelves when all the girls heard a *click*. The central panel of shelves shifted forward. A streak of lightning-quick excitement shot through Skye and she could see it reflected on her sisters' faces.

Had they found them? Could it be that simple?

Pulling hard, the central block of shelves swung away from the wall to reveal a secret recess illuminated in the light from the window. Dust particles danced and swirled in the air, disturbed by the quick breaths of Skye and her sisters.

Summer reached in to retrieve a large bundle wrapped in an old leather sack, dark with age and slightly moth-eaten. As she carefully placed it on the large table the sisters each took a step back, watching it as if it were an unexploded bomb.

Star and Summer looked to Skye, who released the breath she'd been holding, shifted forward and parted the edges of the leather, revealing the contents concealed within.

Disappointment and guilt hit her hard and fast and Skye was instantly reminded of Christmases when her mother's gifts had seemed to be for anyone other than her. But as she looked at the pile of leather-bound books she was crushed that they weren't the jewels that would have made everything so much easier.

Summer took the top one in her hands, carefully, lovingly opening the cover.

'They're journals,' she said, a trace of awe in her voice.

Pressed into the middle of the pile of journals was a small framed portrait of a young girl who looked about five or six years old, around which was wrapped a chain and pendant, tarnished with age. Star took up the loop of silver chain, carefully unwinding it from the portrait, passing the wooden frame to Skye as she continued to study the unusual pendant. Turning the frame in her hands, Skye read the inscription on the back.

Laura, my love
1876—1881

The girl had been five years old. 'This must have been Catherine's daughter,' Skye whispered, overwhelmed by the emotion of discovering their family history and unable to ignore familiarity in the features of the young girl.

'She looks just like you did, Summer, when you were that age,' Skye said with a sad smile.

Summer blinked at her for a moment before turning back to the book in her hands. She cleared her throat a little and said, 'Look at this,' before offering the book for Skye and Star to read.

June 1864
Today was my coming out and everything and nothing was as expected. I know my duty. The need for me to make a match, given that Father has not a male heir. The risk that I should be married off to my cousin doesn't bear thinking on.

Skye sent Summer what she hoped was a comforting smile just as Star let out a peal of delight, her uncontained energy causing the journal in her hands to look slightly precarious. 'This one is dated 1869 and she's in the Middle East! She's talking about elephants and desert castles…'

'We should put them in date order and read them properly. They might contain information about the jewels,' Summer said.

'Why? They're just journals,' Skye replied, feeling bad for dismissing Catherine's memories.

'Journals that were hidden in a secret hiding place never discovered by any of the subsequent generations,' Summer snapped, before instantly looking so sorry that Skye rubbed her arm, letting her know it was okay.

Star ran the necklace through her fingers, holding the pendant close to her face. 'It's a strange-looking thing for the period.'

'And you know much about jewellery in the eighteen-hundreds?' Skye teased gently.

'No, it's just…so *romantic*.'

'What does the last entry say?' Skye asked Summer. 'It might tell us where the diamonds are.'

Checking the dates on the journals, Summer retrieved the last one and turned to the final page and let out a huff.

It has been two days since the wedding portrait and this is where I leave you. There are no shortcuts in life. Already I know that it is the journey, not the destination, that will matter most at the end.

As for my life now? That is for history to document. I chose my path and will make the best of it.

Go with trust and love, always,
Catherine

'Well, that's not cryptic at all,' Skye said.

Summer pulled another journal from the stack and scanned through the pages of neat handwriting—barely a word scratched out, the swirls and loops were pretty on the thin aged paper. Skye frowned when she noticed a letter underlined. Not a whole word, but just a letter. At first she thought it was a mark, a kind of ink blot, but then she noticed another and another.

'Are there any underlined letters on your pages?' she asked Star, who began to flick through the pages.

'Careful! These are over one hundred years old!' Summer scolded.

'See?' Skye said, holding out the journal to show her sisters. 'Here—' she pointed '—and here again. But not every page has them.'

'It's a code. It must be a coded message,' Summer replied with wonder in her voice.

Star sighed. 'This is going to take for ever.'

Hours passed and although admittedly the code was simple, with Summer reading out the individual letters and Star writing them down, there was little for Skye to do other than watch her two younger sisters, who she had almost singlehandedly raised. It had been Skye who had made them dinner and got them to do their homework, got them dressed and to school on time as her mother, more often than not, lost herself to a daydream, or a commune, or a whim. But in the last few years… Well, they were all older now and their lives were taking them in different directions and sometimes Skye couldn't help but feel a little left behind. A little as if she were no longer needed.

'I think I've got it,' said Summer with no hint of tiredness in her voice. 'Here…'

If you have discovered my message then I can assume two things: that you are female, because no man would wade through the private fripperies of my youth, and that you are clever, to have found the journals. That alone makes you more worthy of uncovering the Soames diamonds than my husband.

He has always coveted them. And though society deems him worthy of my hand in marriage, I do not deem him worthy of them. They are the only part of the estate entailed to the female line and I will keep it that way.

Benoit Chalendar, a familiar name if you have read my journals, has the map to the secret passageways—the only copy.

'Chalendar? Why does that name ring a bell?' Skye asked, turning already to her laptop to put his name into the search bar.

'He's the guy Catherine's father commissioned to redesign the house after the fire.'

'What fire?'

'It was pretty bad—it burned down a large part of the original estate that dated back to the six-teen-hundreds. I think it happened just before the journals start. His name came up a few entries into the first journal,' Summer said, before returning to the message.

> *He is the first part of your journey, as he was the first part of mine. We loved—*

Star squealed, 'I knew it!'

> *Yet it was as naïve as spring, though I would not have refused it for the world. He has promised to keep the map safe for you, no matter how long it takes.*
>
> *Good luck, my child. I can almost see you as Laura would have been, brave, loving, intelligent—for you will need all those qualities and more.*

Skye hit enter on her laptop, expecting to see the screen filled with pictures of a man from the eighteenth century, which was why she only took in a chiselled jawline, piercing blue eyes and effortlessly styled sandy blond hair. From *this* century.

'Ooh, nice.'

'Star,' Skye scolded, hating the way that her cheeks stung from a blush caused by exactly the same thought. 'This can't be right, though. He's… he's clearly…'

'Hot?' Summer teased.

'Yeah, but look… This says he's the acting CEO of Chalendar Enterprises. Now, I mean. Not then,' Skye replied, trying to regain control of her senses.

'He must be a relative.'

'He could be anyone,' Skye said, exasperated. 'It's been over one hundred and fifty years since Catherine wrote these journals. What are the chances that he—or whoever Benoit's descendants are—still have this map? And what does Catherine mean, "the first part"?'

'I don't know. It's going to take me some time to go through all these and write out any more messages,' Summer explained.

'Is that a Victoria's Secret model?' Star said, peering over Skye's shoulder, looking at the various headlines proclaiming *this* Benoit as Europe's most notorious playboy. 'Well, I know her—she's an Oscar-winning actress,' Star said, pointing to another one of his reported love interests. Well… not *love*, just 'interests'.

Skye turned back to his bio—the company name rang a bell in her head and then she remembered. 'Chalendar Enterprises—they make high-end building materials. I think Rob's mentioned them a couple of times,' she said, speaking of her boss, once again thankful for the construction firm owner's understanding as he'd let her take this time away from the office. Then again, as her sister had said, she hadn't actually taken a holiday since…since…had it really been five years?

'Is there a phone number for him?' Star asked.

'What—we're just going to call him and ask if he knows anything about a map?' Skye demanded.

'No phone number,' Summer said, looking up from her own laptop.

'Twitter?'

'You want to tweet him?' Skye asked, incredulous. 'What emoji would you use for map and diamonds?'

'There's a number for his office in Paris,' Summer said, reaching for the phone.

'Summer! We need to talk about how we're going to—'

Summer held up her hand, cutting Skye off. 'Hi, yes. I'd like to speak to Benoit Chalendar, please… Oh. Of course. But it's very important that I… Ah. Well, I have urgent contracts that need his signature.'

Skye felt her eyebrows at her hairline. *What*

are you doing? she mouthed to her sister, who shook her concern away.

'I understand, but if these contracts aren't signed by Mr Chalendar, then a massive deal is going to fall through... Which deal?' Summer furiously typed on the laptop, anchoring the mobile between her ear and shoulder, staring at Skye and pointing helplessly at a list of companies Chalendar dealt with. 'Hold on one moment,' she said into the phone. 'What's the most likely "huge deal" that he could be making?'

'Are you insane?' Skye demanded. 'You want me to pick a hypothetical business deal that a man I've never met may or may not be—'

'Just pick one!' her sister hissed.

Skye scanned the list of companies and saw one that did business throughout Europe and America and pointed.

'Hello?' Summer said into the phone. 'Thank you for holding—it's the Stransen Steel contract.' From the loud and clearly panicked reaction from the other end of the phone, it had been a good guess. 'Yes, I'll need an address for the courier... Costa Rica? Two days. Okay. I'll get that done. Thank you,' Summer said, disconnecting the call and tossing her phone on the table as if it had burned her.

'What did you just do?' Skye demanded.

'Found out where Benoit Chalendar is going

to be. But he's only there for two days before he goes "off grid", whatever that means.'

'But shouldn't we find out what the rest of the journals have to say?' Skye asked.

'We don't have time. We have an address for Benoit that expires in two days.'

Star sighed. 'Costa Rica, how rom—'

'Don't,' Summer and Skye said at the same time.

Skye pushed back a strand of hair that had become glued to her temple. The heat was like nothing she'd ever experienced. Perhaps her sisters had been right. She should have dressed more… or, well, actually *less*, given the climate. But she'd wanted to feel in control when she met Benoit Chalendar. So the buttoned-up white shirt and grey blazer, over her jeans and favourite light brown Oxford brogues, had felt like a good idea. Had felt like armour. Until it had been punctured by an eleven-hour flight and a hard dismissal from the man's PA turned bodyguard. He might have looked like a Hoxton hipster but he had been completely immovable. Chalendar would not be seen.

Moisture hung heavily in the air, making it hard to breathe. Her stomach twisted into knots as guilt, shock and desperation clogged her mind. She'd been so stupid. She'd actually thought it might have been that easy. That the man would have agreed to see her. That he would have simply handed over the map.

She searched in her bag for her phone, feeling oddly vulnerable without the luggage she'd left at the airport, having decided to come to find Chalendar first rather than checking in to her hotel. Pulling out her mobile, she bit back the rising sob in her chest and called her sisters.

'What happened?'

Not, *How are you? Did you make it there okay? Was the flight on time?*

'He wouldn't see me. I'm so sorry—'

'Where are you?' Summer demanded.

'I'm outside the hotel, but it's useless.'

'Did you know that Catherine and Benoit had a mad, passionate affair?' demanded Star, as if they hadn't just failed at the first hurdle.

'Yes, I—'

'Skye, you *have* to speak to him,' Summer said, and the urgency in her sister's voice reminded her of exactly what was at stake here. Thoughts of her mother swirled like a mirage in the hateful heat.

'I know, but there's not much I can...' Skye trailed off as she saw a man emerge from the side entrance to the hotel and throw a massive duffel bag in the back of a Jeep. His height was what first drew her gaze. He must have been well over six feet tall but there was a litheness about the way he moved, as if he belonged more in the jungle than a five-star hotel. A honey-blond beard barely concealed chiselled cheeks and a well-defined jaw. It made him look rugged and arrogant, as if he didn't care what people thought. He turned her way and for a second she was caught in the beam of two startlingly blue eyes. An instant jolt ran across her skin and Skye told herself that it was only one of recognition. 'That's him,' she said, forgetting she was on the phone for a moment.

'What's him? He's there?'

'He was…' she replied as she watched him discard her as if she was below his notice and stalk back into the hotel. 'He's putting things in a car.'

'What, now?'

'No, he's gone back inside,' Skye said, exasperated at the running commentary she was having to supply.

'Get in the car.'

'What?' Skye demanded, panic rushing through her. At the thought that she'd miss him, the thought of what her sisters were now screaming down the phone at her.

'Get in the car, get in the car, get in the car!'

'I can't just…' Skye argued even as her feet were taking her towards the Jeep.

'Is it locked?'

'I don't know,' she replied, casting a glance

around her to see if anyone was there to see her trying the handle of the door. Her pulse was racing and a sweat that had nothing to do with the heat broke out across her skin. 'No, it's not locked, but I can't just—'

'Skye, I swear, if you don't—'

'Okay, okay,' she hissed into the mouthpiece of her mobile. Cursing herself, and her sisters, she cast one last furtive glance around to make sure no one was looking. 'This is insane,' she hissed as she pulled open the door and slipped into the footwell of the back seat. A bubble of hysteria rose in her chest, threatening to shut off her oxygen supply. She reached towards the large duffel bag and pulled it over her, still firm in the belief that any second the Hoxton Heavy would find her and demand to know just what she thought she was doing. It was a good question. One she genuinely didn't have an answer to.

'Skye?'

'I'm in, I'm in,' she whispered. 'I have to go. I'll call you as soon as I can.' And with that last promise she hung up, wondering if she'd lost her mind.

'Où est elle?' Benoit demanded, looking around the foyer of the hotel. He didn't have time for this. His staff didn't have time for this. Or at least the

rest of them anyway, he thought, glaring at his assistant.

'Je ne sais pas. Elle est partie.'

At least his assistant had the good grace to look shamefaced at not knowing where the woman he'd asked to leave had gone. Enough for Benoit to know it wouldn't happen again.

Yesterday one phone call to his assistant had upset the contracts team in two countries as they'd scoured through years' worth of Stransen Steel paperwork to find some apparently unsigned contract. He'd received more phone calls in the last twelve hours than he'd had in the last twelve weeks and he'd had enough. He was meticulous with his paperwork, as were the people he employed. This was Stransen's mess and they could deal with it.

'Alors...' Benoit had given this mystery woman enough of his precious time. *'C'est fait?'*

'Oui.'

He left the foyer without another word to his assistant. Four days. He just needed four days of silence, of nothing. No emails, no demands, no company by-laws that forced him into things he never wanted to do.

He checked his watch. He'd wasted at least twenty minutes looking for this woman. Twenty minutes too long. He wanted to be at his home, the only place where he was truly shut off from the world of Chalendar Enterprises—and the axe that hovered over his head.

He'd given everything to the family company in the last fifteen years, but in the last two... He didn't need his great-aunt's warning ringing in his ears to know that he'd pushed himself and—clearly—the board too far.

Shaking his head and biting back a curse, Benoit simply could not believe that he was in this position. That was why he had to get away. To see if there was any way round the ridiculous by-law the shareholders were threatening to enact that meant he had to marry by his thirty-second birthday. Two weeks. He had two damn weeks.

His Great-Aunt Anaïs had tried to warn him, but the final straw had been when she'd mentioned his father. He was nothing like his father. *Nothing.* Before he'd died of a heart attack, André Chalendar had nearly bankrupted the company that had been in his family for more than one hundred and fifty years. And Benoit had brought it back from the brink, he'd made major deals, and so what if he'd immersed himself in a *little* mindless pleasure in the last two years? He was a healthy adult male in the prime of his life and he had healthy adult *very* male appetites. He was single—and would stay that way, no matter what the board of directors wanted.

Refusing to give in to the streak of fury burning bright, he closed the door to his Jeep gently and, turning the key in the ignition, he put the four-wheeler into gear and took the road out of San José. He needed to get to his house before the sun went down. Although the crime rate was low in Costa Rica, the roads at night were a different matter.

He turned up the volume on the radio and let the music soothe him as he glided the powerful Jeep from the smooth motorways off towards the potholed jagged concrete roads that cut towards the rainforest. Four days of uninterrupted blissful isolation was exactly what he needed.

Thirty minutes into the journey he switched radio stations and almost smiled at the heavy base line pounding through his speakers, letting it ripple across his skin and vibrate deep in his chest, when something shifted on the back seat and, heart in mouth, he watched with horror as a figure appeared in the rear-view mirror. Shock caused him to swerve sharply.

He struggled with the steering wheel as it shook in his hands, his muscles tensing against the pull towards danger, and had almost regained control when the car hit a deep pothole which sent it careening off the road and fast towards a tree. He pumped the brakes, desperately trying to slow the car, to lessen the impact, to—

The bonnet smashed into the dense wooden

trunk with an angry shriek of screeching metal and something white clouded his vision and exploded—a popping sound cut through his thoughts, pain sliced his temple and from somewhere he could hear the echoes of a high-pitched scream, realising only a moment later that it had come from the woman in the back of his car.

CHAPTER TWO

BENOIT PUT A hand to his head, where the sting of pain was more acute than throbbing and cursed when he saw the traces of blood on his fingertips. Fighting through the haze in his head, he twisted, ignoring the pain in his ribs, to make sure the woman was okay.

'*Tu va bien?*' he called, hoping that the stowaway in the back of his car would answer.

Nothing, no response. Panic began to build in his chest, outweighing any of his own aches or pains. He was ready to kill her, but first he needed to make sure she was alive.

'*Es tu blessée?*' His breath only escaped his lungs when he heard her groan. At least she was conscious.

'I don't think so,' came the feminine English-speaking voice from the back. 'I just need to—'

'Stop!' he commanded in English as he saw her reach for the door. 'You may have hurt your neck. Just…just stay there.'

Quickly checking himself over mentally, aside from the cut on his temple, a sore—but thankfully not broken—nose from the airbag and an ache in his side that didn't feel like anything worse than bruising, he wasn't too bad. His blood pressure, though, was a different matter. He was probably going to need statins after this.

He kicked at the door from where it had bent shut in the crash and poured himself out of the Jeep. He opened her door and took in the sight of the dishevelled brunette crumpled in his back seat. Stifling a curse, he ignored the wide stare of startlingly rich brown eyes with a sheen that looked horrifyingly as if it might be tears if given the chance.

'I just want to make sure you're okay.' He leaned in and placed his hands either side of her neck, slender and long, the flutter of her pulse quick but strong beneath his palms. She stiffened but held her tongue as he gently pressed. 'Does it hurt?'

'A little, but I'm okay. Really, I am.' The second statement was stronger and, Benoit noticed, irritated. Casting a glance over the rest of her, not seeing any cuts but a whole lot more clothing than was appropriate for the Costa Rican jungle, the woman seemed to be faring much better than he was.

'Okay,' he said, leaning back out of the car.

'Then would you mind telling me who you are and what the hell you think you're doing in my car?' he demanded hotly.

She flinched and the sight caused him to step back. Adrenaline had spiked pinpricks into his skin but as it receded it left an anger he had to get a grip on.

'I needed to speak to you,' she said as she finally struggled out of the back of the car and onto the forest floor beside him. The woman wasn't tiny but she still had to crane her neck to look up at him. 'It's a matter of great importance,' she insisted, her eyes piercing him with a strange sincerity.

Taking her in with one quick glance, he genuinely didn't know where to start. Usually he wouldn't have given her a first glance, let alone a second one. She was attempting to smooth her shoulder-length brown hair into submission. Her body was entirely hidden by a pair of jeans that were neither skintight nor baggy, their only saving grace that they were a pleasant dark inky blue, a white shirt buttoned up to the collar, over which sat a grey blazer that did absolutely nothing for her skin tone. Then again, it was possible the pallor of her skin could be due to the accident. Or because she was English; it really could go either way at this point. Which drew him to her shoes. He didn't think he'd ever seen a pair of Oxford brogues outside of, well, Oxford. Benoit's lips pressed together against the curse that wanted to be let loose.

'Are you from Stransen? Is this about the contract?'

Her eyes rocketed up to his face and if her cheeks had been flushed before then the blush that rose to her skin was almost painful to see.

'Well?' he demanded.

'About that...'

'Yes?'

'It's not exactly... There is... Mmm...'

He watched as she stumbled over her words, wondering whether perhaps she had hit her head in the crash.

'There-is-no-contract,' she said, the words rushing out together so quickly that it took him a moment to mentally translate them.

'What do you mean, *no contract*?'

'Stransen. There is no unsigned contract. We needed to speak to you.'

Benoit paused for a beat that served only to fan the flames of his ire. 'Do you mean to tell me that you had nearly thirty members of staff searching through five years of contracts because you *fancied a chat*?' For once he didn't care that his voice had risen to a shout. Only her lips thinned and it was a look that reminded him a lot of Anaïs when she got annoyed at him and he had a sneaking suspicion that he might just have made a grave mistake.

Fire. That was what he saw when she looked at him next, turning her rich, smooth chocolate eyes to molten lava.

'I will not talk to you like this. You're in a mood.'

'Of course I'm in a mood,' he huffed out through an incredulous laugh. 'We're stuck in the middle of the Costa Rican rainforest, a ten-hour walk from civilisation, the sun is setting and the car is a write-off.'

'And when you're over your mantrum I will happily discuss what I came here to speak with you about.'

'Happily discuss? *Tu es folle.*'

'Did you just call me crazy?' she demanded.

He narrowed his eyes in suspicion. 'I thought the English didn't bother with French past GCSE level.'

'That's both a generalisation and offensive,' she replied, her imperious tone ridiculous given the circumstances.

'And true,' he said under his breath, realising quickly that they needed to stop sniping and get moving. Taking a deep breath, he held out his hand. 'Benoit Chalendar.'

'Skye Soames.'

He hadn't expected her handshake to be firm,

nor for the touch of her skin to cause a snap of unwanted awareness in him. As she removed her hand from his, using it to shield her eyes from a shaft of sunlight he could see the lithe strength in her body, toned yet not overly, naturally healthy and not paid for like some of the women of his recent acquaintance.

'Do you have a phone?' he asked, even though he'd already calculated the chances of having a signal out here very slim. He looked away when Skye bent back into the car, her blazer and shirt rising a little over her backside, gritting his teeth against the shocking spark of a most definitely unwanted arousal.

'No signal,' came the response from behind him.

'Okay. Then we'd better—'

'And you? Does your phone have any signal?'

'I don't have one,' he said, bracing for her rather obvious and utterly expected response.

'What do you mean, you don't have a phone?' she demanded. 'That's shockingly irresponsible.' It was like getting told off by his elementary school teacher.

'I don't have to, nor will I, explain myself or my decisions to you,' he said, walking round what had been his favourite car and prising open the boot. 'Besides, we don't have time,' he said, reaching for his canvas bag and filling it with what they'd need. 'The roads out here are dangerous at night. Our best and only hope is to go. Now.' First aid kit, water, matches, the food he'd picked up at the market that morning. He eyed the bottle of whisky and decided it was necessary. For medicinal purposes, obviously.

He'd known when he'd started to leave his phone behind on these trips that accidents could happen. While part of the attraction was that he would be completely unreachable—no emails, phone calls or anything to do with Chalendar Enterprises—the other part was that it was a test. Of himself. To prove that he didn't need anyone. To know that he could survive using his own skills and his own mind. Of course it usually wasn't a hardship, with his home fully stocked with all his favourite foods and wines. And if he had to walk ten hours through the jungle to get there? He knew he was more than capable. It was Skye he wasn't so sure about.

He turned back to Skye, taking her in as her eyes swept up and down the road. 'Is that all you have with you?' he asked, nodding to her handbag. 'What's in it? Water?' Her face fell. 'Food?' he asked, and it fell a little more. 'Anything?' he demanded.

'No, I… I left my suitcase at the airport before checking in to the hotel because I wanted to see you before you…left,' she said as if she hadn't just hidden in his car to go off to some unknown destination.

'Okay then. Let's go,' he said, hauling the packed rucksack onto one shoulder.

Skye frowned, feeling distinctly unbalanced and unsure. 'I don't... I don't think I should go anywhere with a stranger,' she said, instantly cringing against her own words. Had she really just said that? Maybe she *had* hit her head.

'So you want to stay out here on the road and just hope that a *different* stranger comes to your aid?'

'I have pepper spray,' she said defiantly and then realised she probably shouldn't have admitted it, if *he* was actually someone to worry about.

'Good for you. But this isn't England, the animals here bite and when they do they're poisonous. And that tightly buttoned shirt isn't going to keep them away.'

She couldn't help but self-consciously play with the button of the collar at her neck. 'What's wrong with my—'

'If you don't lose that blazer and undo a button you're likely to lose at least half your body weight in sweat in the next five minutes alone.'

Skye thrust her shoulders back as if readying herself for a fight. 'I don't know you. For all I know you could be an axe murderer!' She'd definitely hit her head and she definitely needed to stop talking. Because she was in complete agreement with the way Benoit was looking at her right now. She was crazy.

'You have no water, no means of making a fire, you have no means of signalling for help and no *real* means to defend yourself.' Her heart was dropping with each and every failing he found in her situation. 'You're dressed like a nun—'

'I'm sorry, I didn't realise you required a dress code,' she interrupted, glad to find something to be angry with him for because then she might not be so angry with herself for getting into this mess. There was nothing wrong with her clothing, she assured herself. But she *was* beginning to get quite hot. 'Would you have preferred sequins, a skirt that barely covers my behind and a pair of stilettos?'

'Personally? Yes. But for now? I would have preferred not to have a stowaway who caused me to crash my car!'

'It wasn't intentional!'

'Oh, so you *accidentally* fell into my car?'

'Yes! No. Sort of?'

'If you can't decide how you got into this mess, how on earth do you plan to get out of it then?'

'Walk,' she said, hating the way her shoulders raised into a shrug and her voice trembled, making it sound like a question.

Benoit stalked towards her in just two strides,

took her by the shoulders and spun her so that she was facing up the road in the direction they had been heading in the car.

'This way, you'll reach the next town in about one hundred and fifty kilometres.' He spun her to face the opposite direction and she tried to focus on the road rather than the way his hands felt on her shoulders. 'That way, you'll reach the next town in about eighty kilometres. Good luck!' he said and stalked off the road and into the jungle.

'Where are you going?' she called after him, feeling for the first time a real sense of fear swirling in her stomach.

'Home,' she heard him growl over his shoulder.

She bit her lip to stop herself from calling him back.

Think, think, think.

She could feel panic beginning to build within her. If she stayed she could be waiting for hours before someone found her. But if she followed Benoit into the jungle it would take her further away from...from... She shook her head. He had the map. He was the key to her mother's treatment. Her stomach twisted as if it had been punched, something she felt almost every single time her mother crossed her mind. He was the only choice.

'Wait.'

He stopped walking, turned slowly and pierced

her with his bright blue eyes. 'Which one is it, Miss Soames? Am I an axe murderer or your salvation?'

She bit her tongue for the first time since she'd got out of the car and he seemed to nod as if he approved of her silence.

'Leave the blazer in the car. You won't need it,' he called out as he set off into the jungle.

Skye threw her blazer in the back of the car, mumbling to herself that if he wanted to have a Bear Grylls moment then he could at least have thought about bringing a satellite phone. But she instantly felt better once the thick layer of her blazer was no longer trapping so much body heat against her skin.

This wasn't who she was, she thought to herself as she followed Benoit through the thick jungle. She didn't get on planes and fly to unknown places, let alone follow strangers into jungles. She was a secretary, for God's sake. She had responsibilities—to her mother, to her sisters. She'd been responsible for them long before her mother had got ill. And would... She couldn't finish that thought.

She almost wished that they hadn't found the journals, that Rob hadn't given her the time off work. Because then she wouldn't be here, so far from everything that was even remotely familiar. Her stomach swirled and she felt a little nauseous. She didn't know what the rules were here, how to act…who to be. Alone with Benoit Chalendar, world-renowned businessman, a supposedly charming international playboy and a man who seemed as at home forging his way through the rainforest as he might be in a boardroom.

He was in front of her, forcing his way through the forest, and she couldn't help but watch the push and pull of his arm muscles rippling beneath his T-shirt as he sliced through another hapless branch. His movements were swift and efficient, his powerful body gliding ahead as if he was in his natural habitat rather than off the beaten path. All the while, heat and humidity pooled in her socks, causing her feet to slip and her shoes to rub. She was being eaten alive by mosquitoes and the sounds of her hand slapping against her skin punctuated the air as much as the thwack of the machete Benoit used to cut back branches from their path.

Hot, Star had said when they'd looked him up on the internet. *Yes*, her inner voice replied assuredly and accusingly—as if Skye had done nothing to feed her body's carnal appetites for far too long… *If ever*, it asserted scathingly.

Benoit Chalendar had been impressive online, but in person? Once the shock of the accident had worn off, and the minutes in the forest trickled into hours, she'd had time to really consider him…or at least the back of him, which was enough. He was wearing khaki cargo pants, which she'd never expected a French billionaire to wear, but they most definitely suited the situation. Strangely, having seen him like this, she just couldn't imagine him wearing some bespoke handmade suit and leather shoes. The idea seemed so absurd she nearly laughed.

The sound she'd made must have caught his attention as he turned back to her, a query painted clearly in those stunning blue eyes. And for a moment she just stared. His sandy blond hair was just a little longer than necessary, curling at the ends enough to make her want to reach out for them. He had a beard, closely trimmed to his cheeks but more than the designer stubble she saw on the backs of magazines at the office. More…masculine.

His nose was a little on the long side but it was challenging, daring the observer to find fault with it, when there was so much beauty in the rest of his features. She shrugged away the unspoken question and he went back to thrashing the foliage, and she went back to…

She hauled her gaze away from his backside and blushed. She barely recognised herself and blamed it on the situation. Because she hadn't actually checked out a guy in… Oh, she thought on a sad sigh, had it really been that long? And the sting of pain as she thought of Alistair, of how he had left, reminded Skye exactly why she had avoided men for so long.

When the first drop of water hit her arm Skye was genuinely concerned that it might have been a tear. But soon there were far too many to count. The heavens opened and in an instant she was drenched. She looked up to where Benoit was standing, beckoning her on with fast movements of his arm.

'Hurry,' he commanded, and this time she obeyed without question. Jogging along the path as best she could, she stumbled slightly when she caught up with him. The rain drowned out the sounds of her harsh breaths as he pulled her deeper into the forest. The huge deep green leaves did little to protect them from the downpour and as she chanced a glance at Benoit she saw that his hair had turned dark with huge drops of water falling from the curling ends.

Her feet were now squelching deep into the mud, her legs having to work even harder to fight the suction beneath her. Her jeans were clinging to her skin, the material stiff and rubbing painfully. A thin branch whipped out and caught her on the arm and she couldn't help the shocked gasp that fell from her lips.

He shouldn't have turned around, he told himself, trying to focus on the thick, rain-soaked foliage in front of him instead of what he saw in his mind's eye. Mud-covered, jeans-clad thigh and white, nearly see-through, shirt slick against a flat, toned stomach. It had taken a lot more than he'd care to admit to drag his eyes up to her face, but that hadn't been much better. She'd just swept her dark hair back, her eyes a little unfocused, mouth open just a little... *Dieu.* All he'd thought was that this was what she must look like when she'd been thoroughly ravished.

He ignored the rush of blood to his cheeks and other areas. It was the heat and the rain and the pace he was having to set. He cast a look back at her to see if she was following. He was surprised to find her keeping pace. Her head was down, concentrating on her steps, only a slight stress on one leg over the other.

He frowned. She hadn't complained once. She'd fought him, accused him of having a... what was it she'd said? He rolled the English word around on his tongue. *Mantrum?* He almost huffed out a laugh. Almost.

He thought fleetingly of what any one of the number of beautiful women to have graced his bed recently would have done in this situation. There would have likely been tears. No. *Definitely* there would have been tears. Maybe even some screams and not the good kind. He'd bet his life on a tantrum or two. But Skye Soames? She was nothing like those women. Not even in looks.

He'd not realised he had a type. Or at least he'd developed one since Camilla, now he thought of it. Just the mental use of his ex-fiancée's name left a bitter taste in his mouth. There was a good reason he'd taken up a penchant for statuesque blondes and his tastes would stay exclusively on those.

'Talk.' He didn't mean it to come out so harshly but she didn't seem offended.

'About?'

'What do you do? Where are you from? How you learned French,' he said as he slashed another branch with the machete. He needed a distraction. Clearly his mind wasn't to be trusted. There was a pause in which the sounds of the squelching mud beneath them and the roaring rain around them became a symphony and he nearly turned his head again but she started talking.

'I… I picked up a bit of French helping my sisters with their homework. And yes, it was GCSE homework,' she said, the confession lifting the corner of his lips. 'And I'm an office manager for a construction firm.'

'Which one?'

She huffed out a laugh. 'You won't have heard of it.'

'Try me.'

'R. Cole Builders.'

In that instant he realised that she'd been right. It was probably…

'It's a small company in the New Forest area.'

'That's where you're from?'

'Mmm-hmm.'

'What's it like?'

'Very different to this.'

'In what way?'

'Do you really want to hear about my childhood growing up in a two-bedroom rented house just outside of Salisbury with two half-sisters, a single mum whose greatest regret was missing Woodstock and an absentee father who started another family as quickly as was humanly possible?'

His feet had slowed, partly because he was consuming all the information she had just disseminated and partly because no one could have missed the echo of pain in her voice. He knew what that was like. Not wanting to talk about the past, parents or childhood. And he had no intention of pressing on that wound. Hers or his.

'I didn't think so,' she answered, misunderstanding his silence. Which was probably just as well. She'd be out of his hair and out of his life as soon as they got back to his house and she could call for help.

He gripped the machete in a tight fist, refo-

cusing on the pathway in front and the sneaking
suspicion that they might have gone off route.

Slash, slash, sweep. Slash, slash, sweep.

They couldn't be lost. He wouldn't allow it.

After five minutes of silence Skye was beginning
to wonder if Benoit was lost. It wasn't that they'd
passed the same tree exactly, but his movements
had become a little…urgent. But perhaps that was
a preferable thing to consider rather than to question why she'd just revealed painfully personal
details to a complete stranger who was probably
not used to more from women than a 'Yes, thank
you, more please.'

She exhaled a long breath. She shouldn't have
been so defensive. She *should* be trying to get him
on side. But suddenly it had all felt too much—
getting to safety, to a phone where she could call
her sisters, to convince Benoit to give her access
to the map, if there even was a map after all this
time. She bit down hard against the urge to give
in to tears. She wouldn't quit. Couldn't.

She followed Benoit into a clearing and came
to a sudden stop, the sight before her cutting off
her thoughts.

'Don't be deceived. It has a five-star rating on
TripAdvisor,' Benoit replied cynically.

CHAPTER THREE

BENOIT STUDIED THE old plane wreck, relief thrumming through his veins. He was soaked through and he wasn't the only one. He'd seen the crash site when out walking on his previous visits and knew that it was too far away from the road to attract unwanted attention.

'Just let me go first.' He didn't mention that there might be things like snakes or poisonous spiders, but they were a real risk. He pulled a torch from his bag and ducked through the jagged hole in the side of the plane where the door had once been. Hitting the torch against the ceiling to scare off any animals, he checked behind what was left of some of the seating of the twin-engine Jetstream and scoured any other possible hiding places he could think of.

Satisfied they were gone, he tossed down the bag and assessed the situation. A fire would be possible—hard, but possible. Though he'd have to be careful what they burned because some of the plane's detritus could have chemicals in it. But there was enough dead wood scattered about for a good few hours of fire, hopefully long enough for them to at least dry off. Nights were dark and cooler than the days, but it would still be warm enough.

But it wasn't really the heat he was worried about. He had to get Skye Soames out of those wet clothes. The way the rain had plastered her clothes to her body was messing with his head and he couldn't afford to be distracted. He cast a look to where she stood outside, her hand at her forehead sheltering her eyes, waiting for his permission to enter, clearly trying to hide the shivers racking her body. Whether it was the cold from the rain, or fear finally kicking in after the crash and the thought of having to spend a night in the rainforest with a complete stranger, he suddenly felt guilty. And Benoit did *not* like feeling guilty.

He called her inside and set about making a fire, not missing the way she perched on the edge of a seat as if ready to flee at any sign of danger. Good. She was learning then.

The smoke from the damp wood wasn't pleasant, but trails of it were finding their way outside through the cracks in the broken windows. Once the fire took hold and the smoke began to clear, he saw Skye shift closer to the heat. The light caught on fascinating strands of red gold in the slowly drying tangles of her brown hair. Hair that rested just above the V in her white shirt, open enough for him to see a tantalising glimpse of…

Scratches. Little angry red lines and an alarming number of bites were already beginning to swell along her slender arms. He stood, not quite to his full height—the angle of the plane's cabin too low for him to straighten fully—and took her in properly, looking past the flare of his unwanted awareness of her to assess the damage the trek through the rainforest and the crash had done to her.

He cursed himself for not realising sooner and reached for the first aid kit in his bag. Opening it, he reached for the one addition he'd made to the small kit a year ago: a bottle of witch hazel. His Great-Aunt Anaïs had instilled a deep respect for the stuff since he and Xander had been kids getting into scrapes at the chateau in the Dordogne. Pushing back the dark thoughts that always followed memories of his brother, he turned back to see Skye twisting her hair in her hand and wringing out drops of water.

He had absolutely no idea why the image of her hair wrapped around her fist shot fire through his body, and if it hadn't been for her cuts and bruises he would have turned his back on her, walked out of the plane wreck and kept on walking all night if he'd had to.

'Here. You need to clean those scratches.'

She looked up at him, her mouth curved into a tight smile. 'And the bites,' she replied. 'I really am sorry about what happened. I must have fallen asleep in the car because I had planned to let you know I was there much sooner. But that's no excuse.'

She'd held his gaze the entire time and he was impressed. The few people he encountered who were inept enough to make mistakes and needed to apologise never met his eyes—instead scurrying to find someone else to blame.

'Let's just make it through tonight and we can figure out everything later,' he said, mentally counting down the hours until they could get to his home and she could phone for...for whatever or whoever would get her back home. He was still determined to rescue some of what would remain of his time in Costa Rica. Alone.

He pulled out a spare T-shirt from his rucksack and threw it to her.

'Change into that,' he said, immediately noticing the steel lengthen her spine at his command.

'What about you?' she asked, her eyes raking over the wet T-shirt plastered to his body.

His jaw clenched, one hundred per cent convinced that she genuinely didn't know what effect that was having on him. 'I guess I'll have to grin and Bear Grylls it.'

The swift intake of breath that followed him out of the wreck spoke of embarrassment and outrage. Good. Much better that than she have any softer feelings towards him. He placed their empty water bottles in secure places to catch the rainwater, while swearing to find out what she wanted as quickly as possible so that when they returned to the house she could leave.

Mortification heated her skin far more efficiently than the fire. The man must have hearing like a bat. He was the perfect predator. Eyesight, hearing, power, looks. Silently growling, she yanked her shirt down her arms and flinched when she heard a tear. She clamped her jaw together, just like she'd done as a child when she'd felt the threat of tears. She wouldn't cry. Not here. Not now.

She was fine. Her sisters were safe. Her mother was happy for the moment and things would look different in the morning. It was only a few hours. Nothing bad could happen in a few hours.

Peeling herself out of the wet jeans, Skye cast a glance around the wreckage of the plane, wondering who it had belonged to and whether anyone had made it out alive. She shivered at the thought. The thin shards of sky she could make out through the cracked windowpanes in the cockpit showed a deepening inky blue. The rain had eased off, but she could still hear the patter of it hitting the body of the plane, which was oddly comforting. Familiar. Unlike every single other aspect of this situation.

The fire had begun to give out some heat and if she hadn't been so hungry she might have fallen asleep. Instead, she hung her jeans, socks and shirt out to dry on various seats and twisted metal and was safely attired in his T-shirt when Benoit returned. Thankfully it was long enough to come halfway down her thighs. If she pulled it down by the hem.

She felt bad as she took in his rain-soaked clothes...until he pulled off his T-shirt and then... All thought stopped. Seriously. He was rich. Clearly defined abs spoke of hours at the gym. This was no lazy billionaire playboy. The dips and grooves expanded and retracted as he reached for something from his bag and when she saw the protein bars in his hand she wasn't sure whether it was her stomach growling or her inner voice purring.

Purring? She *never* purred.

She slapped a cotton pad doused in witch hazel on the bite on her elbow and hoped that the sting would bring her back to her senses. He was digging in his bag with his back to her and for just a moment she indulged in watching the play of muscles in the shadows of the fire. He turned to her with something in his hand and she gasped.

'You're bleeding!'

He frowned, touching his hairline and pulling his hand away with fresh blood on his fingertips. 'It's nothing.'

'It's a head wound.'

'It's hardly a—'

'Sit down,' she commanded, channelling her feelings into anger at him for not saying anything. She swallowed her surprise when he actually did as she'd asked and ignored the wry raising of a single eyebrow.

She came around in front of the seat he had chosen, eyeing the cut that bordered his hairline, leaning and stepping forward slightly to get a better look. He tensed. 'I'm not going to hurt you,' she said, sounding as exasperated as she felt until she reached down to pick up the witch hazel and realised that she'd somehow stepped right in between his legs. Trying to ignore the sudden awareness of...*him*, his chest, his maleness, the heat coming off *all that*, she poured the clear liquid onto a cotton pad before reaching to lift a wave of hair, dark and slick with rain, away from the cut.

She squinted through the dim lighting in the cabin and saw a cut about two centimetres long but thankfully not wide. Cuts to the head always bled profusely, as she'd discovered early on with Summer, whose mind was always on a daydream rather than what was in front of her. And as her mother had a very different idea of what a medicine cabinet consisted of, Skye had become well versed in the use of herbal remedies, even if she'd always longed for proper painkillers and antiseptic cream.

'This is going to—'

'I'm not a—'

The word 'child' that would have come out of Benoit's mouth was cut off as she whacked the cotton pad onto the cut and instead she heard a deeply satisfying hiss. Only then did she realise she was close enough to feel it on her cheek, and somehow on the hairs on her arms and shivering down her spine and shockingly deep within her core.

'I'm surprised to find witch hazel in your first aid kit,' she said, trying to ignore the pull she felt to him.

'My great-aunt,' Benoit said. He continued to look straight ahead with an odd determined glint in his eye. 'She swears by it.'

Skye inspected the wound she'd been pressing on to see if it had stopped bleeding. It was definitely slowing. She took a slightly deeper breath and spoke to the air above his head. 'I'm sorry you got hurt in the crash and I'm sorry about all this.'

'You already apologised. No need for more.' His tone was clipped, but when he glanced up at her something sparked low, igniting quick and hard, rushing every inch of her body in one powerful wave. She'd never felt anything like it and when he lifted his hand upwards she thought for a crazy moment he was going to touch her, until he reached past her to retrieve the T-shirt hung up behind her and all that spark and energy turned harsh, biting and hot, twisting into embarrassment.

As Skye retreated, hiding behind a curtain of gently drying shoulder-length hair, Benoit cursed himself to hell and back. He had more finesse than that. But he'd needed to put some space between them before either of them did something they'd regret.

But for that moment, when she'd stood between his legs with nothing but his T-shirt separating them, his hands had fisted on his knees to stop himself reaching for the backs of her thighs, from running his hands up under the hem of the cotton top and palming—

Dieu, he felt as if his heart was about to explode in his chest. He hadn't been like this since he was a teenager. *It's just the situation*, he told himself. He needed food. And whisky. Not necessarily in that order. He reached for the apple he'd been trying to give her when she'd noticed the cut on his head.

'Here,' he said, catching Skye's attention before throwing her the apple. 'It's not the steak I was supposed to be having tonight, but it's better than nothing.' Leaning over and exhaling through the ache in his side, he retrieved the rest of the bag with the food he'd bought at the market this morning. It already felt like a lifetime ago.

He'd not bought anything substantial, knowing that his housekeeper would have stocked the fridge for his arrival, and certainly nothing that would have been affected by the heat and the journey. So really all they had were some nuts, savoury biscuits, bananas, apples and a few protein bars. It was hardly a feast, but it would get them through.

He divided the rations between them and turned to Skye, who now had one foot on the seat, her arm resting on the knee while the other long, smooth leg, shapely calf muscle and tiny ankle caught the firelight and his attention simultaneously.

Biting down on the apple, she was either the most skilled temptress he'd ever met or completely innocent and Benoit honestly didn't know which would be worse. He'd come to Costa Rica to get his thoughts in order. To figure out a way round the by-law. He honestly hadn't thought he'd need to, sure that the board would eventually back down. But they hadn't. And if he didn't find a wife within two weeks the CEO position would pass to his brother because he *was* married. Reflexively, Benoit gripped his fist, knuckles turning bone-white. No. He'd *never* let that happen. Not after Xander's betrayal.

Benoit had given everything and more to Chalendar Enterprises. When he was a child his great-aunt's words had sunk in and sunk deep. *'We have a duty to the past. A responsibility to bear for future generations to come.'* Benoit had felt the weight of responsibility of a company that had been in his family for over one hundred and fifty years. His whole life had revolved around it, studying applied science, mathematics as well as business, working through summer holidays while at university. He'd worked in every single department they had, learning from the ground up, understanding each part of the organisation. He'd brought the entire company back from the brink of bankruptcy. And the board wanted to enforce the by-law that meant he must marry because he'd had a bit of fun for two years?

But it wasn't just the board, was it?

The crunch of an apple being bitten cracked through thoughts of his great-aunt and brought Skye into focus. Just one day, he told himself. He just had to get through one more day with her.

He passed Skye her portion of the food before reaching for the whisky. He spun the lid from the top and took a large mouthful, swallowing the amber liquid with relish. It hit his near empty stomach like Greek fire and warmed him from the inside out within seconds. He put the bottle down and picked up the nuts, catching Skye's eyes gazing at the bottle on the floor.

'Would you like some?' he offered.

She tucked her bottom lip beneath her teeth.

Temptress.

'I've never actually had whisky before.'

Innocent.

She was giving him whiplash. She'd never had whisky? Who *was* this woman? 'Now probably isn't the best—'

She cut him off with an outstretched arm and a look in her eyes that made Benoit try not to laugh. She had the stubbornness of a mule and he had a feeling that if he didn't comply with her request she'd finish the whole damn bottle just to spite him. And that *wouldn't* be funny.

He passed her the bottle and watched as she took a conservative mouthful of whisky and then struggled not to cough as the alcohol burned her throat. For a second the memory of raiding Anaïs' alcohol cabinet with his brother as kids rose in his mind like smoke from the fire. Benoit's eleven-year-old self had been focused not on the illicit thrill of his first drink but making sure his little brother didn't get sick from it.

Skye finally coughed, shaking her head and flapping her hand by her cheeks as if to dry the big plump tears that he could see sitting in the corners of her eyes. Laughter rose unbidden in his chest and the attempt to stifle it made his shoulders shake, drawing yet another glare from Skye. He held his hand out for the bottle and she passed it back.

'It's not that funny,' she said when she had finally stopped coughing.

'No. You're right, I'm sorry,' he said so insincerely that she threw her apple core at him. Which he caught one-handed and tossed into the fire.

For a while silence descended as they each practically inhaled the protein bars, nuts and fruit. Benoit stuck his head outside to make sure that their water bottles were filling up. If they did finish the whisky the bottle could be refilled with water if it kept raining. Not that it was a good idea to finish it.

Coming back to his seat by the fire, he reached for the whisky, only to find Skye sneaking another drink. He raised his eyebrow and she passed it back to him. He settled back into his seat, took a sip and said, 'So, Miss Soames. Are you ready to tell me why you stole into the back of my car yet? Am I over my "mantrum"?'

'You're not going to forget that, are you?' she asked, a slight trace of humour glinting gold in her deep brown eyes.

'Not any time soon, no.'

Skye fought to keep hold of that feeling. The gentle mockery had built between them, but reality began to bleed in just as the heat from the whisky burned out. She was torn between throwing herself on his mercy and telling him everything, or paying attention to the little voice in her head that said if she revealed everything then he'd have the power. The power to demand anything he wanted, because Skye and her sisters really needed that map. Her mother needed the map. And she simply couldn't trust him not to betray that.

'My sisters and I are doing some research into our family.'

Skye was glad it was dark and that the flames from the fire didn't give off enough light for Benoit to see that her cheeks were bright red. She didn't need a mirror, she could feel them. She'd always been terrible at lying.

'*Oui?* And?'

'And we thought that as your great-great-grandfather did some work on the estate in Norfolk he might have some…relevant documentation.' Oh,

God…oh, God, she was making it worse. Perhaps she should just tell him the truth.

'You came out here for "relevant documentation" on an English estate?'

She reached for the bottle he'd left midway between them and took a rather large mouthful of Dutch courage. It tasted terrible but at least it made things a little…softer? Or was that fuzzier? She wasn't quite sure.

'You should probably take it easy on the—'

'Yes,' Skye said, nodding for emphasis, only that made the ground wobble a little. 'Relevant documentation. Very important. Benoit Chalendar has it.'

'I don't.'

'Not you. The other Benoit. Your great-great-great-whatever.' She could see that he was frowning at her and she groaned. 'He helped redesign the estate after the fire.'

'I know he went to England in the mid-eighteen-hundreds to explore the glass structures at the Crystal Palace before *that* burned down. He was hoping to help develop a stronger, cheaper way of creating reinforced glass. The research he did there laid the way for the future success of Chalendar Enterprises. But I never heard anything about an estate in Norfolk.'

'Of course you didn't.' She waved her hand as if he were an irritating fly, because he was being particularly irritating with all these questions and details. 'It was a *secret*.'

'What was?'

She had the sneaking suspicion that he was laughing at her, but suddenly it wasn't funny. It was important. 'The passageways in between the walls. They were a secret.'

She reached for the whisky, but Benoit moved it before she could take it. She shook her head. Never mind.

'Benoit Chalendar designed secret passage-ways in an English country estate?'

'Yes. For Catherine.'

'Catherine?'

'My great-great-grandmother. Or my great-great-great… I don't know. There are a lot of greats in there.'

She watched as Benoit ran a hand through his hair, continuing to stare at her. She wasn't ex-plaining this very well. It was just that he was so handsome and it was hard to keep it all in her head. But, no matter what, she absolutely could *not* mention the Soames jewels.

'What are the Soames jewels?'

'Are you a mind-reader?' she whispered in shock.

'No. You said that out loud.'

'I shouldn't have said that!'

'Apparently not. Skye, I know you haven't

drunk whisky before, but have you drunk *any* alcohol before?'

'Yes,' she replied indignantly, but perhaps the occasional cider didn't count. 'Anyway, now that you know—'

'About?'

'About the *jewels*,' she clarified, not quite sure why Benoit suddenly seemed not to be so clever at all, 'that Catherine hid in a secret room, locked with a special key, that only the secret passageways can get to. We need the map. Benoit has it. *Had* it? So we thought you had it. *Have* it.'

'You're on a treasure hunt?' The incredulity ringing in his tone jabbed at her.

'Yes. My sister thinks it's *so romantic*.'

'Really? Why?' Benoit seemed to be smiling at her now. With her perhaps? She wasn't quite sure.

'Because they were *lovers*.' She whispered the word as if it were naughty somehow.

Benoit was trying very hard not to laugh. He pressed his fist against his lips to stop himself from making the situation worse because Skye Soames was going to feel all kinds of bad in the morning. But then he was caught by the idea that his ancestor knew hers. Loved hers.

'Catherine's father asked Benoit to review the structural damage at the estate. He believed that a French tradesman would be "of little conse-

access to the map Skye so desperately wanted, then maybe there was a way to solve the problem of the damn by-law.

CHAPTER FOUR

Skye Soames was never drinking again.

She told herself this every single time her stomach rolled or the pounding in her head became particularly acute. What was so great about it anyway? Snippets of her revealing *everything* to Benoit last night crashed through her mind. But, thankfully, she hadn't spoken of her mother's illness. She just couldn't shake the belief that it would put her completely at his mercy.

She was exhausted. She'd always thought that drunk people just passed out, but she couldn't even do that right. Oh, no. Instead of slamming into complete oblivion, her mind had kept racing with Technicolor fantasies of Benoit without his shirt on. In fact, he might not have had anything on in some of the more explicit moments where he'd—

'Are you okay?'

Skye squeaked in surprise, causing him to smirk, which just made her feel worse.

'No, I didn't sleep well.'

'Because of the alcohol?'

'Because you *snore*.'

The sound of Benoit slashing and sweeping through the rainforest came to a sudden halt and she looked up to find him staring at her in horror.

'I do not snore,' he said, sounding so indignant she couldn't help but laugh.

'Oh. You snore.'

'No one's told me—'

'You stick around long enough to have that discussion?' The words took her by surprise as much as Benoit from the look on his face and the racing heartbeat in her chest. Apparently, this was another symptom of the hangover. Or him. She still wasn't sure. Either way, he chose to ignore her question.

Skye flinched as she caught her already ruined shirt on a branch and heard another tear. Back in the plane Benoit had given her privacy to change back into her clothes from the day before and she now hated the pair of jeans that had once been her favourite. They were still covered in mud from yesterday. She'd have given anything for a clean top but that, along with a lot of other things, had been left at the airport with her luggage.

They'd been walking for three hours now and she hoped that there wasn't much more to go. At first she'd been fascinated by the steam rising from the ground of the rainforest, watching it dissipate in the heat of the morning sun. The strange bird calls, feathers fluttering high above them. But the swishing sound of Benoit's machete had now become commonplace and she was sweaty and uncomfortable. It couldn't be too much longer until they reached his home, could it?

She wondered what it would be like and imagined industrial steel and masculine chrome, so very different from her and her sisters' little place in the New Forest. There was space enough for Mum to stay there when she visited, but since Skye had been able to rent a place for herself and her sisters Mariam hadn't liked to be held down by the constraints of a home. She spent her time drifting between friends she'd met on the festival circuits, or other friends with alternative lifestyles. Mum had always been into alternative medicine, but her latest venture was candle magic. Skye loved her desperately, but couldn't see how a candle was going to magic her back to health.

But if she found the map in time, if they found the jewels in time, if the estate could be sold in time…

A branch slapped against her cheek, shock ricocheting through her, and she wondered if Benoit had done it on purpose. For a moment she'd thought things might have thawed between them, and she'd relished the exchange of whole sentences rather than the monosyllabic sparring of their first encounter. But there was a silence between them now that made her uncomfortable. It was so different from the constant noise of her sisters, or the irregular eruptions of the machinery on the building site where her office was in Rob's construction firm.

'So what are you doing out here?' she called out to Benoit.

'You have to ask?'

She sighed. 'No, I mean in Costa Rica. Why have you gone all...*mancenary*?'

'Okay, you're just making words up now.'

'No, it's like mercenary, but without the training.'

'Is this some new form of misandry? Putting "man" in front of a word and making it a term of abuse?' he replied, surprising her, from the look on her face. 'Because I don't particularly care for it. Having never disliked, mistreated or misspoken to, or about, women I'm not sure why you're directing this at me.'

'Did you say all that to get out of explaining why you're in Costa Rica?'

'Did you answer a question with a question to avoid providing an answer?' he fired back, despite the shock sparking in his chest that she'd called him on it. Because no one did that any more. He'd imagined her getting outraged, storming off in a huff and leaving him—as usual—not having to explain himself. Skye Soames, he was beginning to see, rarely did as he expected. But, from the look in her eyes, she wasn't going to answer so eventually he conceded, 'I'm not good in the morning without coffee.'

'You have coffee at the house?'

'Coffee, food, a shower.'

She groaned out loud, the sound making the hairs on the back of his neck stand to attention.

'I'll have the coffee, while eating a sandwich *in* the shower. So...you're here to...?'

Benoit wanted to growl, and not just because she was refusing to give up the interrogation. The thought of her in his shower... He purposefully shut the door on that mental image. She was completely off-limits. If not because of her obvious innocence, then most definitely because of the idea turning in his mind like a screw.

Map. Marriage. Skye. Map. Marriage...

Perhaps he could use her interrogation to at least test the waters slightly.

'To think,' he answered, shrugging a shoulder as if it was nothing. As if the weight of a multi-billion-dollar company and generations of Chalendar men didn't rest upon them. Easing into the subject, he pressed on. 'To get away. The shareholders of Chalendar Enterprises are threatening to enact a by-law regarding the CEO position.'

'Why?'

The simply delivered, innocent questions were beginning to grate. Partly because he knew where they were going.

'Because they don't like the way I conduct my personal life.'

'But if you're not hurting anyone...'

'There is concern about the more salacious headlines being attached to the company name,' he growled.

'It's none of my business,' Skye said, holding her hands up as if warding off any more details or more anger.

'It would be nice if the board saw it that way.'

'How do they see it?'

Benoit clenched his fist around the machete and slashed unnecessarily at the foliage either side of the path.

It wasn't really a case of 'they'. Benoit was one hundred per cent sure the board would have lost the game of chicken he'd been playing with them for the last two years. They knew they were onto a good thing with him as CEO and wouldn't really depose him and risk losing the obscene amount of money he brought to their bank accounts.

'The concern is that negative headlines could affect stock prices.'

You're becoming just like your father.

His great-aunt's words had been like a sucker punch. He hadn't seen it coming. It had dropped him to his knees. He felt it even now.

'Are they right?'

'What?'

For a moment he feared she was asking him if he *was* becoming just like his father.

'No. I don't think they're right to be concerned about stock prices. But what I think doesn't matter. They are going to vote on it at the next meeting.'

A meeting that Anäis had called. The reality of it simply blanked his mind. It stopped all thought. As if Benoit simply couldn't comprehend how she, of *all* people, could do that to him—could betray him like that, could threaten to take away the one thing—

'And what is this by-law?'

'It requires me to get married or step down as CEO.'

'That's crazy,' she replied.

'No more crazy than searching for a one-hundred-dred-and-fifty-year-old map of secret passage-ways and hunting for missing jewels,' he bit back angrily, mentally at war with the need to defend his great-aunt whilst also cursing her. He was the only one who could do that.

'No, I mean what's crazy is the assumption

that marriage would suddenly stop you being a philanderer.'

'Philanderer?'

'Would you prefer another description? Playboy, womaniser, Lothario, rake, libertine—'

'You're having too much fun with that,' he growled again. 'You'd think they'd have learned their lesson last time. It's not as if it worked with my fath—' He bit off the word, clenching his jaw, shocked that he'd even half said such a thing.

After a pause, he heard Skye ask, 'So when does this marriage have to happen by?'

'My thirty-second birthday.'

'Which is…?'

'Two weeks.'

'And if you're not married by then?'

'The company goes to my brother, who *is* married. And I'd rather see the whole lot burn in hell before I let that happen.'

Once again silence descended, occasionally punctuated by the thrash and thwack of Benoit's machete. Skye had been surprised by the anger in his voice when he'd spoken of his brother. No matter what had happened with her sisters, no matter how hard she'd had to push them to do their homework or go to school, no matter what she'd given up for that to happen, she could never imagine feeling that much anger or...*hatred* towards either of them.

She checked her watch and realised that it had been twenty-four hours since she'd last spoken to them. Without a signal she hadn't been able to contact them last night, and this morning her phone's battery had died. The thought of being out of contact with them, with her mum...it was like a thousand spiders crawling all over her.

Were they worried about her? Would they try to call the hotel that she hadn't checked into? Would they try to contact the Costa Rican consulate? She thought of Summer, probably nose-deep in one of Catherine's journals. Of Star, daydreaming about exotic far-flung places. Of her mother, who knew nothing about the journey they were on. They'd decided against telling Mariam any more than that they were stuck in Norfolk sorting out the terms of the will, not wanting to get her hopes up, or remind her of painful encounters with her father. But, beneath the rambling roll of her thoughts, Skye had buried deep the fear that they weren't worried about her. That perhaps they weren't even thinking about her at all.

Benoit began to cut off to the left and soon Skye realised why. She felt an inconceivable amount of excitement when she saw a crumbled concrete road through the dense foliage and jogged to meet him. They shared a victorious smile as they reached the tarmac and pressed on. Without the protection of the rainforest the sun's heat was unbearable but the prospect of his home spurred them on. He pointed out the glimpse of a dark roof off to the left, but it wasn't until they rounded the last twist in the road that Skye finally saw the house.

Wow.

Nestled into the side of a hill within the rainforest, the building sprawled in deep mahogany lines and large planes of glass reflected nothing but the shapes of leaves and trees. It had two tiers perching along the hill's gradient, framed above by a large flat square of concrete that looked suspiciously like a helipad, the shape mirrored harmoniously below by an azure blue pool lined with trees to provide shelter and seclusion.

It took her the final fifteen minutes of their walk just to take it all in. It was the most beautiful construction she'd ever seen. The use of materials perfectly blended with the setting, but not just that…it was the detail. The finish. It was flawless. Rob would have probably dropped to his knees and wept to have seen such a thing. She was on the verge herself with the prospect of finally getting to a phone and speaking with her sisters. Once she knew they were okay, that Mum was okay, then she could talk to Benoit about the map.

She followed him through the front door, her eyes wide, expecting magnificence. She wasn't disappointed. She took in everything—the incredible mezzanine floor book-ended by the most breathtaking floor-to-ceiling window she'd ever seen, creating a wall of green trees, leaves, plants and wildlife. The ground floor was large and open-plan; the kitchen and dining area were along one side and the sitting area was set at a slightly lower level. Skye couldn't help but spin in a slow circle, trying not to feel overwhelmed by its opulence.

The furnishings were modern classic with touches of industrial materials mixing well with the natural wood and glass. Somehow the monotone shades suited the bright rich greens from the rainforest surrounding the house, ensuring that the natural artistry of the location was displayed to its fullest. Skye was drawn to the side wall of the sitting area—the entire length and breadth covered in rows and rows of book-covered shelves all the way to the ceiling. A stair ladder hung from rungs along the very top shelf. She had so many questions. But there was only really one to ask.

'Can I use your phone?'

Benoit stilled just as he was putting his bag on the kitchen countertop, his whole body taking on the solidity of the concrete beneath her feet.

'You cannot use yours?' he asked.

'My phone died last night, and my charger is in my suitcase back at the airport. Look, if you don't want me using your phone, that's fine. I'll just borrow your charger.'

She frowned as she realised that he was looking at her oddly.

'You don't have a charger,' he repeated slowly.

'No,' she said, unsure why he suddenly seemed so…weird.

'When I said I come here to get away, I meant to Get Away. From everything.'

'And?' she demanded, beginning to feel a little irritated.

'Everything includes phones, mobiles, internet…and phone chargers.'

'What are you trying to say?'

'I'm not trying. I'm saying. There is no way for anyone to contact me here. No way for you to call—'

'We're stuck here?' she demanded, the realisation finally sinking in.

'Until the helicopter arrives in four days' time to pick me up? Yes. We're stuck with each other.'

Forty-five minutes later and Benoit's ears were still ringing. He must have told her one hundred times that it couldn't be kidnapping if *she* was the one who'd got in his car. And the suggestion that her panic might be down to hunger had apparently been akin to saying that she was hormonal. She'd screamed. Actually, it had been more like a growl. Though, Benoit thought, that must be an English thing because he was starving and it was making him as angry as she appeared to be and he had no problem admitting that.

He winced as he heard the slam of one of the bedroom doors as she tore through his house, refusing to believe that his house was 'off-grid', as she had taken to calling it, or that he was that 'irresponsible', as she had taken to calling *him*.

'What if there was an emergency and your family needed to contact you?' she'd demanded.

His reply that they would send a helicopter hadn't appeased her.

'What if *you* had an emergency and needed help?'

His suggestion that he'd deal with it had been met with scathing disapproval.

'What if you fell down the stairs and couldn't move and were unconscious?'

He hadn't liked the way she'd looked at the long set of stairs to the first floor—as if she'd like to push him all the way down and test her theory.

He watched Skye come down the staircase and without a word pass through the large glass door that led out to the patio. And then he sighed. Because he did feel a bit bad for her; he wasn't a complete monster. She'd survived a car accident, a night in the Costa Rican rainforest, himself in the morning without coffee, only to arrive at their destination and discover there was no escape.

He picked up the cafetière cups and took them out to the table on the patio. He sat, trying to focus on the peace his garden usually brought him, but his attention snagged on the hunched shoulders of Skye Soames.

'I don't have time for this,' she said, facing away from him.

'I know the feeling,' he said grimly, thinking of the days counting down until his birthday.

'No, I mean I really... I can't be here right now. I need to be back home. I was supposed to be back home by now.'

Once again, Benoit couldn't quite shake the feeling that there was something that she wasn't telling him. Usually he wouldn't care, but there was something about her tone, something that snagged in his chest.

'What back home is so important?'

Everything. But Skye couldn't tell him that.

'Your sisters?' he asked.

She nodded, knowing that it was only half the reason she felt so panicked. She turned and joined him at the table. He tentatively pushed a cup of coffee in her direction, as if worried she might throw it over him. But she gratefully scooped up the china in her hands, her mouth watering at the rich scent and hopeful that it might help stimulate a few more neurons so that she could find a way out of here. She'd been surprised to find that Benoit had been telling the truth.

No phone. No internet. Nothing.

Her heartbeat thudded heavily in her chest as she battled with the panic in her mind. She couldn't be stuck here. They didn't have the time. Her mum didn't have the time. Each hour, minute even that she didn't have the map, that they weren't closer to finding the key, or the passageways, felt like a minute stolen from her mother's life—and that thought was paralysing.

'How old are they?'

'Twenty-four and twenty-two.'

He huffed out an incredulous breath. 'From the way you were speaking, I thought they'd be much younger. They'll be fine,' he said, instantly dismissing her concerns.

'It's a lot for them to deal with—' she tried to justify herself '—and Star? Well, she'll probably fall into some romantic notion about whatever the next step is to find the Soames diamonds and Summer will probably forget to eat because she'll be lost in Catherine's journals.'

'Skye, Star and Summer?'

'Mum's choice.'

'Not your father's then?'

Skye shrugged, ignoring the ache suddenly blooming in her chest, blotting out some of the panic, not quite sure which was the lesser of two evils. She drew her coffee cup to her chest as if it could ward off the question.

'Mum left him when I was about thirteen months old. She didn't like his normal, main-stream lifestyle.'

'And he just let you all go?'

'Well, he let me go. Star was born after an affair and Summer doesn't know who her father is. Don't get the wrong idea—it's not that Mum was…like that.'

He frowned. 'I'm not judging,' he said, raising his hands in defence.

'Everyone judges,' Skye assured him. 'I learned that pretty quickly.' Teachers, parents, school friends.

I don't want her playing with my child.

But Margaret, she's my daughter.

And that's fine. For you. But she runs around here like a wild thing, with barely any clothes or care, and it's not the way I will raise my son.

Skye hadn't thought about the conversation she'd overheard between her father and stepmother for years. It sent a shiver down her spine, despite the thick damp heat of the forest around her.

She'd stopped talking about her childhood and

her sisters when she realised a woman with three children by different men was called names. And the children? Her and her sisters? They didn't escape either. But with Benoit she genuinely hadn't felt such censure and it was an odd feeling.

'Look, why don't you have a shower? I'll leave a towel and some clothes out—they'll be mine, but better than what you have with you. I'll stay inside until you're done,' he offered, standing up from the table.

A shower sounded amazing. She was contemplating the opportunity to get out of her two-day-old, sweat-soaked, muddied clothes, when she registered his words fully. 'Stay inside? Where's the shower?'

He nodded over to the corner of the patio. Of course this man would have an outdoor shower. *Of course* he would.

She heard him disappear into the house while her mind registered the implications of showering outside, naked amongst the elements where anyone—or Benoit—could see her.

It's just a shower, Skye, she told herself sternly, disliking the way even the thought of it made her feel exposed, vulnerable…but hating the way it also sent a thrill rushing through her. As if it were something illicit, guiltily pleasurable. A thrill that she welcomed for blocking out all thoughts of her father, of her mother, her sisters…

She cut a glance to the shower and slowly pushed back her chair and made her way towards it, staring at it as if it were a challenge to her 'conservative' lifestyle—something her mother always bemoaned. Mariam Soames would have loved it.

Benoit returned with a towel and the clothing he'd promised before leaving again, but Skye waited for a good few minutes before she made her way across the decking towards the stunning outdoor shower surrounded by huge green leaves offering a sense of privacy. Small mosaic stones and turquoise-coloured tiles covered the floor in a beautiful pattern.

Toeing her shoes from her feet, her heart was racing to a different rhythm, a lighter one, faster. The idea that Benoit could—at any moment—catch a glimpse of her naked under the jets of water made her feel…*alive.*

She peeled her jeans from her legs, half fearful, half desperate to get rid of the clinging denim. Now that he wasn't in front of her, her mind raked over and indulged in memories of Benoit by the fire without his T-shirt on. The way his shoulders had seemed like organic boulders, large and powerful, the sandy blond trail of hair dipping below the waistline of his trousers.

The blush that rose to her cheeks stung in its intensity and she doused her heated skin with an icy blast of water from the shower. Only instead of soothing her fevered imagination, it inflamed. As she ran her hands over her body, in her mind they belonged to Benoit and it was making her want things she never had before. Certainly not with Alistair, her one and only boyfriend.

She turned beneath the spray, the sight of something glinting in the forest further down the hill cutting off the direction of her thoughts. She frowned. That couldn't be right. Benoit had said there was no one around here for miles. But then again, he hadn't mentioned the motorbike she'd found in the garage either.

Had he lied to her?

Skye turned back to the rooftop she'd seen glinting in the distance. It was definitely a house. Surely they would have a phone. Knowing there was no way she could stay here for four more days, she reached for the towel and fresh clothes before she could change her mind.

Benoit was hiding in the house from the temptation that was Skye Soames. The house wasn't very big but it was definitely clever. His ears strained for the sounds of the shower and he realised he hadn't heard it running for a while. In fact, he hadn't heard anything for a while now.

Frowning, he risked a glance outside his bedroom window and couldn't see her. Unease stirring in his chest, he scanned the spare rooms on the mezzanine floor and made his way downstairs. Not seeing her on the lower floor, he went out into the garden towards the shower, where the floor was still wet from use.

He looked about and, catching sight of the roof of his neighbour's house, he ran to the garage. His motorbike was gone.

He cursed out loud. She was going to get herself killed.

Or worse—ruin his damn bike.

CHAPTER FIVE

THE WHEELS SPUN on the hot tarmac and Skye grappled with the evil machine as it threatened to shoot off once again without her. She was shaking with fear and it wasn't helping her control the bike, but she was determined to master the thing.

She'd made it at least two miles before she'd had to wobble to a stop when she'd hit one of the many cracks in the road and nearly toppled the whole thing over. It had been half that distance since she'd last seen the roof of the neighbour's house but the road kept twisting her in the wrong direction and she was beginning to worry now.

How on earth did people ride these things? Underneath the shower she'd felt rejuvenated and determined but the road was dusty and having a go on Alistair's moped seven years ago hadn't seemed to have given her any real ability to handle Benoit's motorbike.

She took in a shaky breath and told herself that she could get control of this blasted machine, of this damned situation. She had to. She desperately wanted to speak to her sisters but, more importantly, she didn't want to turn back, humiliated and shame-faced, and see that *I told you so* look on Benoit's face.

With trembling hands, she twisted the bike's handle, her heart momentarily soaring as the engine spluttered into life, only for it to buck and stall beneath her, knocking her off balance. The weight of the machine pulled her downwards and she and the bike crashed to the ground, hot metal digging into her calf muscles and pressing her skin into the gravel on the road.

She slammed the floor with her free hand and let loose a curse. 'What am I doing?' she demanded of herself.

'I was about to ask you the same question.'

She gasped out loud as she saw Benoit bearing down on her, his body so imposing it blocked out the sun. How could she be both relieved and terrified at the same time? Except she couldn't quite put a name to what she was scared of.

Benoit hauled the bike off her, righted it and, putting it on its stand, checked it over for damage. He remained silent but she could see the way he clenched his jaw, the muscle flaring again and again. She didn't have to justify herself or her actions to him, she thought defensively. Only…she had stolen his motorbike, probably damaged it, just like she'd damaged the Jeep.

Oh, God, the repair costs! She hadn't even thought of that. She was barely covering rent, let alone the contributions to Summer's university expenses. If they didn't find the map and the diamonds she'd be in debt to Benoit up to her eyeballs, and her mother...

Skye bit back the sob that was about to rise in her chest.

'I'm sorry,' she said, to Benoit and to her sisters. She'd let everyone down. She felt the hot press of tears behind her eyes and blinked desperately, hoping they wouldn't fall. 'I'm sorry,' she said again. 'I don't know what—'

'You saw the neighbour's house and the bike and thought I'd been keeping it from you. *Chérie*,' he said, finally turning to pin her with a gaze the colour of frost, 'do you think I want you here? Do you think I like the idea of sharing these four precious days—the *only* days in my whole calendar year that I'm not at the beck and call of emails or meetings or contracts?'

She bit her lip to stop it from trembling. Benoit spun around but barely spared her a glance before pacing back and forth with clenched fists.

'If I'd thought my neighbour was there I'd have taken you. If I thought there was enough gas in the tank of the bike to get us anywhere near a

phone or civilisation I would have taken you. If
there was any way I could have got rid of you,
Ms Soames, I swear to you I would have taken it.'

Benoit was furious. But he was also relieved not
to have found her in any serious trouble. The
fear and anger he'd felt when he'd found the
house empty... A shiver worked its way up his
spine, and only now was the tension beginning
to ease. Scouring the house for any sign of her
had reminded him of the way his brother had run
through the house the morning after his mother
had left them. The slicing pain in his heart as he'd
seen the moment Xander had realised that their
mother had gone and left them behind.

Something Benoit had already known since
the night before.

'Are you sure they're not at the house?' she
whispered, making him feel bad. Which made
him feel angry all over again.

'He's never at the house. But I can see that
you don't trust me, so come on,' he said, ignoring the twist in his gut as he realised it was true.
'Let's go.'

She frowned, casting a glance over his sweat-
soaked shirt and the rapid rise and fall of his
chest. 'How did you—?'

'I ran,' he growled forcefully, slowing his
breathing, its rapid pace having nothing to do

with exercise or his anger. The moment he'd seen the bike on top of her… It just didn't bear thinking about. She ignored his hand and got up by herself, so he turned and swung a leg over the seat of the bike, pulling it to standing. 'Get on.'

'What?'

'Get on. We're wasting daylight hours and I don't fancy another three-hour walk in the rainforest, do you?' he asked pointedly.

Benoit held the bike in place as she tentatively stepped towards the machine she'd nearly destroyed. She was dressed in the clothes that he'd laid out for her. She'd rolled up the sleeves of the white linen shirt; the smallest one he could find was still large on her. It was tucked into the tan cargo shorts, which were cinched at the waist by the belt she'd worn previously, but the legs hung so low that they looked like culottes on her. There were a few inches of creamy, delectable calf and slender ankle on show before her tan Oxford brogues. How on earth she'd made the outfit look even remotely stylish was lost on him.

He felt her settle into the seat behind him and couldn't help but roll his eyes as he waited until her hands were around his waist. Finally, when she'd exhausted every other option, he felt them, but she'd pushed herself as far back as she could get, which would topple them the moment they took the first corner. He reached behind him, hooked a hand behind each of her knees and tugged her against him, holding back a curse as he felt her slender thighs encase his own, the press of her breasts against his back. It wouldn't be for long. He could control himself in the less than ten-minute ride to his neighbour's. He had to.

He glanced at the fuel tank and prayed that they'd make it back home. He was done with trekking roads and jungle with this woman, especially when there was no whisky to make it at least a little enjoyable.

The thought reminded him of her missing jewels. The search for a map that had brought her out here in the first place. Last night it had seemed amusing, like a campfire fairy tale. But now, with the sun beating down on them and Skye's desperation as clear as day...

Something strong and sure told him that if the map existed then Anaïs would have it, would have kept it all these years. He could recite the words she often said by heart. *We have a duty to the past. A responsibility to bear for future generations to come.* He felt them as if they were written on his soul, had always been.

He hadn't worked eighty-hour weeks for nearly fifteen years just because he wanted to prove himself better than his father, or to fill the devastating sinkhole he'd made in the company's finances. He'd done it because he'd felt the weight of the ancestors *before* his father. The ones who had given blood, sweat and tears for Chalendar Enterprises. Because they deserved more than his father. He'd done it for Anaïs and even now, when she was threatening to take it from him, he'd do it all over again. Because Chalendar Enterprises was the only thing in this world that—unlike people—wouldn't let him down.

The company that in two weeks he'd have to hand over to the brother who'd betrayed him because Anäis no longer trusted him. Benoit revved the engine, momentarily forgetting his purpose until he felt Skye shift slightly behind him.

Skye, who was so desperate she had flown halfway across the world, stowed away in a stranger's car, stolen a motorbike she clearly didn't know how to ride…

A desperation he could use to his advantage.

Skye shielded her eyes against the rays of the sun as if that would suddenly allow her to see signs of life in a home that looked more like a prison. It was a foreboding concrete block of a house, so different to Benoit's. Instead of sympathetically echoing the surrounding nature, it stood out like a sore thumb. Angry and out of place.

As Benoit leaned the bike on its stand she rested her hands on his shoulders to lever herself from the seat and wobbled unsteadily on aching legs before finally coming to stand on her own. No. A second look did not reveal any more signs of life, other than a red blinking light next to what looked like a security camera. Perhaps…

'Don't even think about it.'

'What?' she asked innocently, as if she wasn't considering criminal action to get what she needed. Maybe she *was* going crazy. That, or she'd inherited a little more of Catherine Soames' adventurous nature than she'd realised. But there was a thin line between adventurous and reckless.

'If you do that you'll end up in jail for breaking and entering—which, I assume, was the next stage of your plan. And as much as I resent your presence here, I don't think I'd like to see you in a Costa Rican jail cell. Because that's what will happen. And then you and your sisters really will be in trouble.'

Anger spiked through her then. 'Don't use them against me.'

'Why? It seems to be the only thing that will get through to you.'

'It's just that I'm… I'm…'

'Feeling out of control and hating the fact that there's nothing you can do about it,' he cut in.

'Would you not finish the end of my sentences?' Her shout was consumed by the dense concrete and live green foliage surrounding it.

'Fine,' he replied, tight-lipped and grim-faced.

She knew that he was right. She couldn't break into someone's house to see if they had a phone. She might have ticked reckless behaviour, theft and destruction of private property off her criminal to-do list, but she couldn't add breaking and entering to the list. Even for her sisters.

Benoit was right; the neighbour wasn't at home and he really hadn't exaggerated the situation. There was no way out. Not until his helicopter arrived in four days' time.

'It is only four days,' he said, his tone for the first time neither mocking nor angry.

Four days.

Just four days. Skye knew that in the grand scheme of things it wasn't a lot of time. Even with her mum sick, it wasn't long. And really, what could Summer and Star get up to in ninety-six hours? She couldn't fight it, couldn't carry on like this. It was exhausting and damaging. She had to trust that they would all be okay. She *had* to.

'Are you done?' Benoit asked Skye the moment the resolute energy holding her up seemed to drop away and she sagged in defeat.

'Yes,' she replied as a wave of exhaustion threatened to pull her under and she dropped onto the seat behind him. This time she put her arms around Benoit's waist without a second thought, her body sinking against his as the speed of the bike picked up and the air rushed through her hair.

She allowed her mind to completely blank, to simply relish the sensations around her. The cool rushing air against her skin, the feel of Benoit's torso beneath her fingers, the shift and sway of the muscles of his back against her chest, her thighs reflexively tightening around his as they turned a corner… She closed her eyes and leaned a cheek against his shoulder blades, losing herself to the sensations of the bike's movement, rather than those of her fevered imagination. When she next opened them, Benoit was slowing the bike at the gate to his home.

He walked the bike into the courtyard and leaned it on the stand. He waited for her to slither off the seat before he gracefully swung his leg over and stalked off into the house. His silence was beginning to really eat away at her and she hurried after him, having gone from wanting to flee to feeling as if the only safety she had was when she was with him.

'Where are you—'

Her question stopped short as she watched, eyebrows at her hairline, as he started to strip off his T-shirt.

'Shower,' he growled, looking at her as if daring her to comment.

She bit her lip and watched as he stalked

through the French windows, grabbing a towel he must have left there earlier. She pulled her eyes away the moment his hands reached for his waistband.

Instead she turned to the kitchen and, with her back firmly to the garden, she focused on the contents of the fridge and not what was happening outside. In the shower. Where, in the gathering dusk, stood a very naked Benoit.

Food. They both needed to eat. And although she wasn't completely comfortable rummaging around in a man's fridge, it was the least she could do. The list of debts she was accruing with Benoit was getting longer and longer by the minute.

As she marinated steak and chopped cucumber, lettuce, tomatoes and whatever else she could find to go in a salad, the twist and turn of embarrassment that gripped her like bindweed wouldn't quit. She was embarrassed by her actions, by the train of her thoughts. By the way she'd reacted to the feel of her hands wrapped around his waist. A low thrum at her core reminded her that it hadn't just been the vibrations from the bike she'd felt, that the heat hadn't just been from *his* body, and…

And then Benoit walked through the French windows, emerging from the shower with just a towel around his waist and water droplets darkening the sandy blond hair curling around his head. She nearly dropped the knife she was using to cut the tomatoes.

Her eyes drank in the sight of him, the ripple of his muscles as he stalked towards her, her mind thankful for the barrier of the breakfast bar between them, her body crying out in frustration. The power of him, the predatory look in his gaze as he allowed her to take her fill of him unabashed, unashamed. Her skin sizzled in response; the thin flame of need turned into a wildfire storming through her body. She yanked in a jagged breath.

'You should not look at me like that unless you have every intention of finishing what you're starting.'

His words hung between them, the challenge ringing loud, clear and utterly undeniable.

Skye looked away, pretty sure she heard him say, 'I thought so,' as he made his way up the staircase to the second floor.

By the time Benoit was dressed he told himself he was back in command of his libido. She'd clearly had no idea what that look had done to him and he wished *he* didn't. Because it was interfering with the now fully formed plan in his mind. The one that said Skye Soames was the answer to his problems. And the reason that she was perfect was not just because she desperately needed the map that he was convinced his great-aunt had hidden away, but also because nice girls like Skye Soames didn't go for bad boys like him. In fact, he fully expected her to find his proposal so outrageous it would cut that attraction dead. Which was good, because he had absolutely no intention of messing up the only decent solution he'd found to this entire situation with something as fleeting as sexual desire.

Feeling a familiar sense of complete self-belief in his plan and its success, he snagged a bottle of wine before heading out into the garden where Skye had laid the table and placed the steaks.

She had waited for him but when he took a seat she barely met his eye.

'Would you like a glass of wine?' he asked.

'I don't think—'

'Not that I want to pressure you into drinking, but it's a light wine and you can stop at one glass. You'd be drinking with food so...'

'The effects won't be as potent as the whisky?'

'Pretty much, *oui*.' He smiled, hoping to put her at ease, and to completely ignore the passing comment he'd made on his return from the shower earlier, even though the words still burned his tongue. 'This looks delicious, thank you.'

After he took his first bite she seemed to gingerly approach the steak and spear the smallest piece with her fork. She stared at it a long time before putting it in her mouth.

'Is something wrong?' he asked. She shook her head, slowly chewing and eventually swallowing.

'No, it's just... I...haven't eaten meat in five years.'

Benoit nearly spat out his wine. 'What? You're vegetarian?' he demanded.

'It's not that shocking.'

'I'm not shocked by the vegetarianism, but that you'd suddenly decide to eat steak!'

'Well, it's not me that's the vegetarian. Summer became vegetarian five years ago and Mum's been vegan for years, so it just seemed easier if we all did.'

'Skye, there are plenty of vegetables in the fridge!'

'I know. But you missed out on your steak last night. You said so... And, given how much trouble I've been...the Jeep, the bike... I can't even imagine how much I owe you,' she said, still not meeting his eye.

'You don't owe me anything,' he said sincerely, not once having given thought to charging her for the damage. Instead, he was searching Skye's face for traces of the determined, no-nonsense woman who'd trekked through the jungle covered in scratches and bites. He rubbed his forehead, appalled that she had just broken her principles to appease him.

'Please, Skye, don't eat any more of it,' he said, the small bite he'd already managed sitting heavy in his gut.

She looked up then, gold flecks flickering in her brown eyes. 'Actually,' she whispered as if confiding a secret, 'I really like it.' And she took another mouthful of succulent meat. And another. And another.

She groaned in appreciation and Benoit fisted his cutlery in his hands, trying to shake off the realisation that this woman had spent years denying herself pleasure when he never refused it.

'I'm sorry. I genuinely support vegetarianism. I wholeheartedly believe that it's both better for our digestion as well as the environment,' she explained, eyeing up another forkful.

'These were sustainably sourced, I assure you.'

'Thank you. I appreciate it, I really do. But every once in a while…it makes you appreciate and value the meat you do have.'

'Will you regret it tomorrow?' Benoit asked, genuinely curious. Rather than fobbing him off with an answer she seemed to give the matter some thought. She looked into the distance over his shoulder, squinting a little as if working through possible consequences. Once again, he was struggling to fathom how she had put her own wants—something as simple as the occasional piece of meat—aside for her sisters. As a man who had luxuriated in giving into his every selfish want in the last two years it was a strange notion.

'No. I don't think so. It doesn't mean that I'll call my sisters and tell…' She trailed off, clearly remembering that she couldn't just pick up the phone and call them. 'But I knew what I was doing when I chose the steaks for dinner,' she pressed on.

'So the vegetarianism was…?'

'My mum,' she supplied. Benoit couldn't be sure but there was something in her eyes…as if she both wanted and didn't want to carry on the conversation. 'Mum's lifestyle is…*alternative*. It's a wonder we all survived childhood.'

Benoit was thinking that it probably had more to do with Skye than a wonder.

'What's she like?' He was clearly tired as usually he would never have allowed himself to voice such a personal question. But he couldn't deny that he was curious. Something about this woman was niggling at him. Like a puzzle that he wanted to solve.

Skye smiled but again that smile… It was…sad?

'She's loving and enthusiastic and creative, but not the most down-to-earth. She is truly a free spirit.'

'And you're not?'

'No, it's just that when you're a child, school and homework and clothing are actually mandatory, not just *governmental interventions on parenting and free will.*'

'She's a nudist?' he asked, the image of the self-contained, conforming Skye in front of him and the free-living and loving picture she was painting jarring in his mind.

'No—' Skye laughed '—not really. She just values her freedom to be how nature intended, freedom to love who she wants, be how she wants. But in reality that doesn't quite work when you have three children to drag into adulthood.'

Or two. Because Benoit had the distinct impression that it wasn't her mother who had nurtured her children into adulthood but Skye.

Anger ignited in his gut and it took Benoit a second to get a hold on his feelings. The power of them had taken him by surprise while Skye seemed oblivious. In his mind's eye he saw his mother, the look on her face as he had caught her packing her bag that last night.

'Is it cooked okay?'

'Yes. Very okay,' he said, forcing an answer to numb lips as he returned to the present. He smiled belatedly and she cocked her head ever so slightly as if sensing something was wrong.

'I've been thinking about your map,' he said,

forcing a change in subject and his mind onto the goal he should not have strayed from. 'The only person who might be able to help is my Great-Aunt Anaïs.' Even if their last parting had been heated, Benoit knew her love for him was as undeniable as his love of her and not even Chalendar Enterprises would change that. Especially if he found a way to keep it, despite her attempts. 'Anaïs is all about family duty, honouring the past to secure the future. She's also devious enough to have kept something like that a secret from me this long,' he said, a smile pulling at his lips.

'You love her,' Skye noted.

'You sound surprised? Of course I do. Anaïs took care of us after our father's death. Two orphaned teenage boys, as wilful as we were wayward.'

'Were?' she said sceptically.

'You think I'm wayward?' he replied, trying to avoid the truth of his past but knowing he couldn't. 'Our childhood was different to yours. My father might not have left, but sometimes I wonder if we would have been better off if he had.'

'Don't say that.'

She was right. He shouldn't have said that. Shouldn't have revealed as much. If there had been a thought that she might have understood… it disappeared like smoke.

'When the helicopter arrives,' he said, getting himself back on track, 'it will take me back to France, to the Dordogne where Anaïs lives.'

'And you'll take me?' The hope shining in her eyes was startling. For a moment he didn't want to douse that hope. But he had a company to save.

'That's up to you.'

'Why?'

'Because I have a proposition. One that you'll need to think seriously about before agreeing,' he said, his eyes locking with hers, confirming the seriousness of what he was about to say.

'What proposition? You know I have nothing to give you,' she said, frowning. 'And I doubt you need money.'

'Not money. I don't need that. But I do need a wife.'

CHAPTER SIX

SKYE STARED AT Benoit, waiting for him to laugh and tell her it was all a joke.

'You can't be serious,' were the only words to escape her lips.

'I am,' he said, his blue eyes hardening like ice. 'I have something you want—' the dismissive shrug of his shoulders just plain irritated her '—and you could be something I need. It's a simple exchange.'

'Exchange? It's not an exchange, it's a *marriage*,' she couldn't help but cry, her mind scrambling to process everything, her mind racing as he offered the one thing she needed and then pulled it from her reach. 'You're barbaric.'

'No, it would be barbaric to kidnap you and force you to marry me, but I'm not. I'm offering you a deal—'

'A deal?' she demanded, horrified at how quickly Benoit had turned from someone sharing confidences to contracts.

'You don't have to take it.'

'But we need the map,' she insisted.

'And I need a wife,' he said determinedly.

'Find someone else,' she begged.

'I don't have time.'

'But you *did* have,' she accused.

'Honestly, marriage is the last thing I ever wanted, and I truly thought I'd find a way to manipulate the board.'

'And instead you manipulate me?'

'It's easier,' he said as if he really didn't care.

She'd been about to tell him about her mother. To explain why it was he shouldn't have wished his father had left, no matter what. To try and share how precious life was, even if that relationship was flawed... And now? There was no way. This was not a man whose mercy you could hope for.

Her heartbeat pulsed in her ears.

Thud, thud, thud.

It felt like the seconds marked by a clock. Time running out. For the jewels, for her mother. And, horrifyingly, she could already feel herself wavering—her mind running over the possibilities, the steps that could be taken.

'This is crazy.'

'You want a way to control the situation—well, this is it. I'm offering you a way to take back that control.'

'By handing it over to you?'

'I wouldn't be that kind of husband.'

'And I refuse to be that kind of wife,' she said mulishly.

'Then the helicopter will drop you back at the airport, where you can get a flight home and you can explain to your sisters why you will never have access to the map.'

'Now that definitely sounds like blackmail,' she said, pushing back from the table, her half-eaten plate easily discarded now that her stomach was in turmoil. She stood and walked to the edge of the pool, casting a look about the dark shadows of the rainforest but not seeing it. Instead, she imagined her sisters in the library at the Soames estate, poring over Catherine's journals, trying to find the next clue in the search. She saw her mother in her friend's back garden looking over the New Forest, counting down sunsets that she had left. All the while Benoit waited. Waited for her to come to the same conclusion he had. That there was no other option.

She shook her head as if trying to deny what she knew she had to do. There must be another way, she thought. 'Why do you want the company so badly?' she asked in the hope that his answer might offer one. 'Surely it can't be the worst thing for your brother to—'

'I'll never let him have it. He's taken too much from me already.'

Once again Skye registered the darkness behind his words when he spoke of his brother. And for the first time since he'd dropped this shocking proposal like a bomb between them he wouldn't meet her gaze. This time *she* felt like the predator, waiting and watching, looking for signs of weakness. He had used hers against her and she was determined to repay the favour.

'Explain,' she demanded.

'No,' he scoffed.

'It clearly has something to do with this "deal" of yours and I would like to consider all angles—'

'There are none,' he growled.

'I'm sorry if this dents your ego, but if there's a way I don't have to marry you I'll take it,' she returned angrily.

His eyes turned even more frosty and a chill ran down her spine as if it had been touched by an icy finger.

He glared at her one last time before looking out at the rainforest over her shoulder. 'I was engaged once before,' he said, his voice grim and his jaw tight. 'Camilla was the daughter of a business associate. We met five years ago and within weeks it seemed like the perfect match. She was impeccable, poised, understood my need to focus on the company. Or…that's what I thought at the time. For three years we courted, Camilla reluctant to move in with me until we were married. I had proposed, but I was holding out on the wedding—I wanted everything in place, everything perfect. Xander and I were selling off one of the subsidiary companies to focus on the research and development side of things.

'Research and development was something I'd always wanted to do. My father had no head for science, nor finances, and under his tenure the company had gone to the brink. I wanted the company to get back on track, to work on building a foundation that was more than just about supply and demand of building materials. I wanted us to be *leading* the demand. There is so much that can still be done, different ways to make the materials. Cheaper ones that could be of benefit to the world as well as the environment, instead of mindlessly using what's already there despite now knowing the impact and the harm.'

She heard the pride and ambition in his voice. The passion. In some ways she felt it was the truest thing she'd heard him say. Felt it call to her because it met a yearning within her that she'd never been able to fulfil. Not while looking out for Star and Summer. And when he returned to the story of what had happened in the past, the light went out of his eyes.

* * *

'I'd been distracted by a big new contract and Xander had been distracted by something else. He'd grown withdrawn and uncharacteristically antagonistic. I was relieved when a trip to Hong Kong had been cancelled at the last minute so that I could see him and get to the bottom of what was going on. I wanted to make sure he was okay.'

Benoit huffed out a bitter laugh. 'I went to his apartment…' His words conjured memories he hadn't allowed himself to examine for two years and in his mind he retraced the steps up towards his brother's door. He watched himself retrieve the spare key to the apartment from his pocket, knowing that he should knock, perhaps even then sensing unconsciously that something was wrong.

As he'd walked down the hallway he'd known, he thought now. Because why else would he have pressed on, why else would he have rounded the corner to his brother's bedroom, when any sane person would have turned back? He'd ignored the signs in the kitchen and dining room—the glasses, the empty bottles of red wine…

'I found them. In bed.'

Even now bile rose to the back of his throat. The sight of Camilla in a red lacy body suit dressed for seduction churned his stomach. He remembered how she'd shifted, leaning back, and the moment that he'd locked eyes with Xander.

The pain, guilt and anguish he'd seen there lost to the horror and outrage exhibited by Camilla.

'Rather than owning any sense of shame, she became a harpy, screaming and accusing.' For some reason all Benoit could call to mind was the flash of her bright red nails—the colour matching her lingerie—nails that had seemed more like talons that night. 'She told me it was my fault. That I had taken too long to get married. That Xander was everything that I wasn't.'

'And your brother?' he heard Skye ask, her voice filtering from the present into the past.

'He didn't say a thing. He didn't have to. He knew. I knew.'

Knew that the trust had been broken. And they would never get it back. Even now Benoit hated that the anger was mixed with an agony he daren't name, let alone acknowledge. And he would certainly not dig deep enough to investigate why it also made him feel a little less guilty.

Turning his back on the past, he looked at his future. Skye.

'I'm truly sorry that happened to you. I can't imagine what that kind of betrayal would be like,' Skye said. 'But is marriage really the right way to ensure the company stays with you?'

'I didn't tell you this for your sympathy,' he bit out. 'I told you to make you understand that there is no alternative. My hand has been forced by my family—something I believe you are familiar with—and I will not let you near the map unless you agree to be my wife. Now, it's getting late and I, for one, am looking forward to sleeping in a bed tonight.'

Skye looked around as if she'd only just noticed that the sun had set, the stars had risen and the day had turned to night.

'I don't have an answer for you, but I won't forget that you twisted my arm into this.'

'Good. You shouldn't. Don't forget, *never* forget, the one thing that can be trusted in life is that when everything is on the line, selfishness will always win out.'

Skye woke to the sound of Benoit's words on a loop in her mind, his accent and the softly spoken words at complete odds with the sentiment.

Selfishness will always win out.

And then she remembered his other words. *I need a wife.*

And I need the map, she thought.

She couldn't see a way round it. Benoit was the only person who could give her access to Anaïs, who *had* to have the map. And they needed the map to find the jewels to sell the estate if they were to have any hope of raising the money for the treatment Mariam needed so badly. For just a moment she had considered telling him about

Mariam. About the cancer that was ravaging her body and how the only treatment they could get was freely given to others but would cost them the earth.

Or her hand in marriage.

Selfishness will always win out.

She just couldn't trust him not to use it against her. So no. She would *never* tell him about her mother.

She pulled back the covers of a bed so comfortable it had been like sleeping on a cloud. She went to stand in front of the window that formed the entire wall of the bedroom, just as it did below. The night before, the view had been a dark velvet cloak punctuated with silver sequins. Now the sight of the rainforest was magnificent, an endless stretch of green, making her feel like the only person on the planet.

She found her bag in the corner of the room where she'd dropped it yesterday, beside another shirt and a pair of lightweight trousers she *hadn't* seen yesterday. She'd have expected to feel outraged at the idea of Benoit in her room while she slept, but the image of him looking down on her while she'd been unaware… She shut down her errant thoughts.

This was a man who was trying to coerce her into a marriage she didn't want.

As she showered, she realised it didn't matter.

Even if he wanted her to stay with him in France and never set foot back in England, even if she never saw her sisters again, Skye knew without a shadow of a doubt that she would do *anything* if it meant her mother would get the treatment she needed. If it helped the girls to find the jewels that would also secure their futures.

Even marry a complete stranger.

Only Benoit didn't *really* feel like a stranger. The only thing that had seemed strange about him was how cold he had become the night before. It was as if telling her about his ex-fiancée, about his brother, had drawn all the warmth from him. And she couldn't help the part of her that wanted to give him the benefit of the doubt. Because he was the man who had dismissed thousands of pounds in damages, who had been worried about her when she'd disappeared with his bike, who had been almost distraught at the idea she might have eaten meat on his account. And he was also a man who was clearly devastated by the hurt caused by his brother two years ago.

Dressed in the clothes that Benoit had left and the set of clean underwear she always carried in her hand luggage whenever she travelled, Skye followed the scent of coffee all the way to the patio outside.

Benoit was sitting in the same chair as the night before and if he wasn't wearing different clothes she might have thought he hadn't moved. His eyes were closed, his face turned up towards the sky and the sun. He seemed truly relaxed for the first time since she'd met him. There were slight crinkles around his eyes, but not as if he spent a lot of time laughing; rather that he spent a lot of time squinting—as if suspicious, or calculating.

The short beard was getting a little thicker, tempting her to wonder what it would feel like beneath her fingers. Soft? Rough? The way it framed his bottom lip, the full flesh casting a shadow from where it crested seemed carelessly sensual.

'Do you want some coffee?'

Skye jumped and couldn't help the cry of laughter that escaped at her own silly reaction. Her heart pounded in her chest and she felt tingles running all over her skin in relief as the spike of adrenaline crashed out of her system.

'You scared me,' she accused, taking the seat opposite Benoit, who still hadn't opened his eyes.

'You shouldn't sneak up on people.'

'*I* wasn't the one sneaking around.'

He opened one eye and peered at her. She gestured to her clothing, which she instantly regretted because the heat that burned beneath the places where his gaze raked was indecent.

'Would you rather have gone about naked? Or, worse, in yesterday's clothes?' he queried.

'I'm not sure you have that in the right order.'

He shrugged as if he didn't agree with her.

Despite having rolled up the dark blue linen trousers, the material kept unwinding to fall about her feet. But they were cool in this humid heat and, as Benoit pointed out, clean. She'd used her belt again to hold them in place, but somehow doing so had made her think about him, about the way his torso tapered down...

'Terms,' she said out loud, startling them both. 'We need terms,' she reaffirmed.

'So you agree? To the deal?'

'On one condition.'

'Yes?'

He'd nearly said, *Name it*, but that would have told her how much he needed her to agree. He hadn't realised how unsure he'd been of her answer. The night before, memories of the past had made him overly harsh and some alien inner voice told him to stop now before it was too late. But a darker one was already relishing victory.

Skye Soames was too sweet for this. She'd probably already rationalised his behaviour, finding some reason to justify his ruthlessness. But he had given her fair warning. *Selfishness will always win out.*

'I get the map first.' Skye's demand cut through his thoughts.

'No.'

'Yes. I have time constraints.'

'Which are…?'

'Immediate,' she replied, not answering his question as he'd have liked, nor meeting his eye. She clearly didn't like being evasive. He could use that.

'How immediate?'

'More immediate than your birthday.' This time she was looking straight at him. In her eyes he could see a firm line. This, she wouldn't budge on.

'*D'accord*. When we return to France I'll take you to Anaïs and we will attempt to find this map of yours. Then we will marry.'

'Wait? France? No. I have to get back to England.'

'Not until after we are married.'

'Hold on—'

'Skye, let me make this incredibly, painstakingly clear to you. There is no way I'm going to let you have the map, should it exist, and leave, just trusting that you'll come back.'

'But I give you my word.' Her insistence was sweet, but definitely naïve.

'Sadly for you, that is not enough,' he said. 'For all I know you could be an axe murderer,' he replied, throwing her once hotly issued words back at her with a shrug of his shoulders. 'So. You can have the map, photograph it and send it to your sisters. You can courier the thing for all I care. But you will not leave France until we're married.'

He could tell she was buying time. She managed to stretch out pouring a single cup of coffee. Then she spent an inordinate amount of time picking her breakfast from the feast of fruits, pastries and yogurts he'd assembled before she'd come down from her room.

He watched her hand sway over a *pain au chocolat*. It went back and forth and, curiously, eventually back to her lap, leaving the pastry where it was. There was something about that he didn't like. It frustrated him that she would refuse to allow herself something she clearly wanted. It angered him, he realised, as he reached across the table, picked up the *pain au chocolat* and put it decidedly on her plate.

'I—'

Benoit cast her such a look—he might even have growled—that she immediately stopped what she'd been about to say. 'If this is another thing, like the vegetarianism, I don't want to hear it,' he commanded.

Skye folded her lips between her teeth and picked the corner of the flaky pastry, popping it into her mouth. She chewed slowly at first and then reached for another piece, then another until finally she picked up the whole pastry and started to take proper mouthfuls.

He picked up his coffee and looked out into the distance, away from where Skye's slender throat was working, clenching his jaw *again* against her gentle groan of pleasure that sent sparks down his spine and made his stomach curl. He cleared his throat, trying to block out the sound and restore his equilibrium.

'I have terms of my own,' he managed to bite out. As she was still enjoying the croissant, he took her raised eyebrow as an invitation to continue. 'This,' he said, gesturing between them, 'will not evolve beyond this deal.'

She blinked. Then she swallowed. Then she squinted. 'You mean…?'

'No romantic notions, no daydreams of a happy ever after, no—'

'I get it,' she interrupted before he could say any more. 'That won't be a problem,' she went on as she removed a flake of pastry from the corner of her mouth with her thumb. He watched every single second of her doing so. 'So what would this actually look like?'

'Real,' he replied more quickly than he'd have liked.

She locked her gaze onto his. She seemed to bite back a sigh. 'How do you see it working?'

In all honesty, Benoit wasn't sure he *had* seen it working. He'd fully expected her to tell him to go to hell.

'I need to be married before my birthday, which is two weeks away. I know that you have business to attend to, so afterwards I wouldn't expect you to be chained to my side,' he said, his vivid imagination stumbling over the image of metal loops and wrists and... 'But the board would need to believe that the marriage is real. And my family are the board of Chalendar Enterprises so it will have to look good. There is, however, not a length of time stipulated by the by-law. Perhaps because it was written when marriages were expected to last.'

'So we would divorce?'

No, he thought, but couldn't quite explain to himself where that had come from, so instead replied, 'Yes.'

'How long?'

Benoit shrugged, aiming for a nonchalance he really didn't feel. 'Three years.' He'd meant to say two.

Skye choked on her coffee. And not just a pretty throat-clearing for effect. Flakes of pastry and coffee caught in parts of her throat they shouldn't have been in, produced a considerably violent outburst.

Three years seemed impossible. She didn't even—

The thought stuttered to a halt, but Skye forced herself to face it. She didn't even know if her mother would be here in three years. The almost constant sob caught in her chest, throbbed. But if Mariam Soames wasn't alive in three years, then did it really matter what Skye's world looked like then?

'Water?' Benoit offered as if he didn't know that he had been the cause of her choking.

'No,' she said, clearing her throat. 'No, thank you. Three years…' she said, turning over what that might mean in her mind. 'You'd be celibate for three years? Really?' she said, her errant thought escaping before she could stop it.

Now it was Benoit's turn to look shocked.

'Explain,' he demanded.

'It might not be a real marriage, but I'm assuming there will be a fair amount of public scrutiny at the news that a well-known international playboy…' she pushed on past the scoffing sound he made '…is getting married. And I have absolutely no intention of being humiliated while you are repeatedly photographed with your latest plaything.'

'Plaything?' he repeated.

'*Not* the point, Benoit,' Skye replied, knowing that she would stand firm on this.

'And you?'

'What about me?'

'All things being equal, you would also be celibate for three years.'

'That...that's fine,' she said, suddenly not liking the way the focus of this conversation had turned back on her.

'There's nothing *fine* about it,' Benoit returned hotly. Honestly, Skye really didn't know what he was getting so worked up about. The one time that she'd had sex with Alistair had been...had been...well, *fine* and she just didn't really know what all the fuss was about.

He was staring at her now as if there was something wrong with her and she didn't like it. It was the same way she'd felt when she'd overheard women talking about sex as if it was something incredible—as if she were missing something. Life was so busy that she'd not really had a chance to make close friends and there was *no way* she was talking to her sisters or mother about it. Her mother, who thought that sex was a divine right, that bodies should be worshipped and that love was something that was better shared with as many people as possible.

Oh, God. She wanted to put her head in her hands. She was a twenty-six-year-old prude.

'We can talk about this later,' she said eva-
sively.

'Oh, no. We're talking about this now. We'll
have other things to talk about later,' he warned.

'Why—are you going to demand that I share
your bed if you're not allowed to find others to
do so?'

'Don't be crass. I wouldn't do that to an innocent.'

He said the word with such distaste that it took
her a moment to realise what he was saying.

'Wait—you think I'm a virgin?'

'You're not?' he asked, just as shocked.

'No!'

Skye didn't know why she was so offended.
There was absolutely nothing wrong with being
a virgin; it was just that she wasn't and she didn't
like him thinking that she was. Was that really
how she came across? But now he was looking
at her as if he couldn't quite work her out.

'Who was he?'

'No one important.'

'Clearly.'

'I didn't mean it like that. And I have no intention of sharing that with you.'

'Skye, we're going to have to get to know each
other *very* well if we're going to fool my family
and the Chalendar board that we're in love and

getting married. And if you can't even tell me about a boyfriend then—'

'Fine, but not now.'

'You have something better to do?' he asked, as if amused.

'Yes.' *No.* She just had to get away from him. She didn't like the way she felt when he looked at her like that. As if he saw…*into* her. She pushed the chair back from the table, stood and nearly tripped right back into it when her foot caught on the long hemline of Benoit's trousers.

He reached out an arm to steady her, the muscles of his forearm corded and powerful; she looked from there to his face and his eyes…frosty blue shards flaring in the sun. She pulled herself back upright, rubbing at the spot on her arm that prickled from where he'd held her.

He'd let her off. She knew it and he knew that she knew it too.

CHAPTER SEVEN

IT SHOULD HAVE been easy to get lost in a house several times the size of the one that Skye shared with her sisters, but it wasn't. She was acutely aware of Benoit the entire day she tried to hide from him. First, she'd gone back to her room but there was absolutely no chance of her falling back to sleep again. Then she'd wanted to go for a shower but Benoit was still outside, having been for a swim, just soaking up the sun like a seal. Sleek and wet and…

Stop it!

Then, when she'd ventured downstairs to the bookcase that stretched all the way up to the ceiling and ran the entire breadth of the house, she'd been overwhelmed by choice. There were thousands of books. She ran her fingers along the spines, awed by the sheer number of crime novels, biographies and architecture and design books. She found a thriller she hadn't read and turned to go back upstairs but Benoit was cutting through the open living area so she dropped, sinking into the plush sofa, hoping that she hadn't been seen.

She lost herself in the story of a misanthropic British secret agent two years from retirement, stalking his arch nemesis through Westminster and London to Moscow and eventually Paris. She missed the sounds of Benoit making lunch in the kitchen, missed the sounds of her stomach growling as she turned each page. She couldn't remember the last time she'd had the luxury of getting lost in a book, without worrying for her sisters or her mother.

An ache she'd been ignoring for far too long rose within her. Usually she was too busy with work, with the house, with checking on Star and Summer and her mother to pay any attention to it. But here in the stillness of Benoit's Costa Rican paradise, with no distractions, it was getting harder and harder to ignore.

The suspicion that she hid behind all those things swirled like steam within her, thick, damp and sad. Sister, daughter, secretary, *parent*… The suspicion that she hid in those roles because they gave her purpose. They gave her a sense of identity, something she had lost when she had been torn between two vastly different households and ended up feeling as if she quite fitted into either of them.

She'd been so young she'd barely even had a sense of who she might be when it had seemed far easier just to be something else. The perfect, well-dressed daughter for her non-confrontational father, the stand-in parent for her half-sisters, the sensible, practical daughter for her mother—the mother who did exactly what she wanted, was exactly who she wanted to be, not having to conform to the rules because Skye was there to do it for her.

But who did Skye want to be?

'It's a good book, Skye, but it's not *that* good,' Benoit announced, cutting through her thoughts and the sob that had half risen in her chest. He placed a glass of wine on the table in front of her that looked red and rich and her mouth watered.

She looked up, startled. Night—it was night again?

'You've been reading for about eight hours.'

'Eight?'

'Yes. Hungry?'

'All I do here is eat and sleep and—' She broke off, looking at Benoit's broad, encouraging smile. 'What?'

'That is the point.'

'Of your escape here?'

He gave a deep sigh as he sank into the corner of the large L-shaped sofa, the breath expanding a chest clearly defined by a lightweight dark wool sweater over a white linen shirt. 'Yes. To completely switch off and recharge. There isn't always time in France.'

'Why Costa Rica? Why not the Caribbean or Monaco or…?' she asked, genuinely curious.

'Some other generic playboy destination?'

'Yes! That, exactly,' she replied, enthusiastically warming to the teasing, perhaps too much, desperate for a distraction from her thoughts.

Benoit leant his head back against the high arm of the sofa so that he was looking up at the ceiling. She hadn't meant it to be a probing question, but she realised in an instant that she had pushed his thoughts to a part of his past that he didn't want to go.

'My brother and I used to play forts. Anaïs would pack us lunch and we'd run off to the woods for the entire day, building fires, exploring. I loved it. I thought I'd be an explorer one day. But every time I'd ask where Xander wanted to explore next. It was always the same—'

'Costa Rica,' they said together, Skye smiling at the sweet story.

But it was a sad smile he offered her in return. 'I think even then we were making ourselves scarce from our father. He was…' Benoit struggled to find the right words to describe him. 'You never knew what mood he'd be in. He was charming and irrepressible when he was in a good mood, but most of those good moods were spent with other women, outside the home. And when it was bad he would rage through the house, berating us or our mother for some imagined slight.' The memories of those times rose up around him. His father's spiteful shouts, red-faced rage and fury were something he rarely dwelt on. 'He could be paranoid and furious. It's partly why he was so dangerous as CEO. The board thought that a wife and family would settle him, but I think we only made it worse. He had a marriage of convenience with my mother. I'm sure that she didn't know what she was getting into, which is why she chose to run away.'

He had spent so much of his childhood protecting Xander from his father, from his mother's absence. So yes, he knew something of what Skye felt towards her sisters. But he also knew what it had felt like when all that sacrifice, all that protection was turned against him, betrayed. Since the night his mother had left he'd always tried to protect Xander, to look out for him, to bear the brunt of his father's fury. Only for him to sleep with Camilla.

'What happened to your mother?' Skye asked.

'She died about two months after she left—a car accident in Italy.'

'I'm sorry.'

'Don't be—the family will expect us to know

things like this about each other.' He knew that wasn't what she had been apologising for, but it made it easier to circumnavigate the solid ache in his chest. 'It's good; we need to know more about each other, so keep asking.'

He looked up at her. She had her feet tucked under her and a light throw over her lap. She seemed to fit, as if she'd always been here at the house. The reds in her hair blended with the dark wood and the paleness of her skin echoed the pale walls. She was a thousand textures. Smooth, soft, sharp, strong...

'Why did you think I was a virgin?'

His eyes snapped to hers in surprise. That was *not* what he'd expected her to ask. Her fingers were playing with the throw and it was clear she found the question deeply uncomfortable. He could lie to her. It would have been easier, for her and for him. Less...dangerous. But that wasn't his style.

'You don't seem that in touch with your sensual side,' he said, wondering if it was a trick of the light that made her cheeks seem to flush. 'You don't seem very aware of that part of you. You dress like a secretary.'

'I *am* a secretary. Well, office manager, but...'

He smiled. 'But you weren't working when you came out to Costa Rica to meet me. It's more than the clothes though. It's...' he waved his hand towards her and shrugged '…it's the way you are,' he said, avoiding the simple truth he felt to his soul.

'What is it? Just tell me,' she said, finally meeting his gaze.

He clenched his jaw. 'You don't behave as if someone has given you pleasure.'

Skye clamped her teeth together to prevent whatever reaction was welling up within her from escaping. Because she didn't know what would come out. Embarrassment, anger, hurt, arousal, cries, screams, sobs. She felt it all.

She might as well have been a virgin.

'Alistair was…we were young.' Why was she defending him? Because they had been young. They hadn't known better. Not really.

'How young?' Benoit demanded hotly.

'Not *that* young,' Skye said with a small smile at the strange kind of protectiveness that seemed to be on display. 'He just…'

'You were pressured?' Benoit had gone very still.

'No. Not in the way you think. We'd been together for the last two years of school. I don't even know what he was doing with me, even now. We hardly saw each other; I was so busy with Summer and Star and school. And he'd been patient and kind and understanding.' Sweet. It had felt sweet. 'But when it came time to leave school, to move onto the next stage in our lives, he thought I was going with him to London.'

'You didn't want to?'

'I did. But Summer was starting GCSEs, Star her A-levels. I couldn't go. He was hurt, sad. And...' She shrugged, unable to find the words as an adult, the ache in her chest, the awkwardness clogging her mind.

'You slept with him because you couldn't go with him to London?'

'I wanted him to have something that he wanted,' she said, heat in her cheeks. It seemed wrong, looking back over the distance of time.

'But did you want to?'

'Yes,' she replied. She'd wanted *him* to have that.

'You shouldn't make a gift of yourself like that. Your sexuality, your pleasure—that's not something to give away. You can share it, but you must have it for yourself at the same time.'

'Do you need to know anything else about him or are we done?' Skye forced the words out.

'You can ask me anything you like,' he said, his tone immediately lighter, for which she was eternally thankful. Because what he'd said had made her warm, ache, hurt and happy all at the same time.

'Your girlfriends? No, thanks.'

'Really? You don't want to ask me *anything*?'

'Not particularly. Though…the headline about the sisters… No. Actually, I don't want to know,' she said, laughing as she reached for the glass of wine on the table. It tasted dry but fruity on her tongue and she wondered whether it was just because he had an exquisite wine collection or he'd chosen it for her.

'What about your parents?' Benoit asked, studying her gently over the rim of his own wine glass. 'You said your mum is a free spirit?'

'Yes. The full package—tie-dye flowing skirts, flowers in her hair, the festival circuit. Her head is in the clouds but her heart is bigger than anyone's I've known,' she said, smiling at the memory of Mariam Soames dragging them out of school to play with them in a wildflower field, but feeling sad that she hadn't been able to fully enjoy it because she'd been too worried. About what the teachers would think. About what her father's new wife would think. She had been so torn. She ached to think of what she had missed. If only she'd been able to fit in with her mother and sisters just a little more.

'And your father?'

'A professor.'

'Of…?'

He clearly wasn't going to let her get away with one-word answers.

'English Literature. They met at university in London and had a passionate affair before Mum decided that "university education was riddled with the not always unconscious bias of male upper-class oppression".'

'She too doesn't like the patriarchy?' Benoit teased.

'Etymologically, patriarchy means a structure of rulership distributed unequally in favour of fathers,' Skye explained, slightly wincing at the tone of her own voice, but unable to stop. 'So I'm with Mum on this; universities are not skewed in favour of fathers, so I didn't mean patriarchal.'

His smile at her response hit her square in her chest. 'Where did you go to university?'

'I didn't,' Skye said, frowning and pulling at the thread on the beautiful throw covering her lap. She really shouldn't, she told herself. It might completely unravel.

'Really? Why not?' The surprise in Benoit's voice stung as much as it pleased. She liked that he'd thought she'd gone to university.

'We didn't have the money.'

'A university professor couldn't put his daughter through school?' He sounded half confused, half outraged.

'Dad remarried and he and his wife wanted to…decided that…' She hated that she was stumbling over words. It shouldn't be this hard just to say it. 'They put their money towards their son's education.'

'What?'

'It's fine,' she said to him in the same way she'd said to her mother, and to her father when he'd told her that he wasn't able to help. Even though he was able to; he and his wife had just chosen not to.

'It's not. What kind of mother is she?'

'Good, from what I can tell,' Skye replied honestly. 'She's a loving, perfect, stay-at-home mum who was on the PTA. The kind of mother who packed her son's bag the night before school, never forgot lunch, helped him with his homework and always remembered indoor shoes as well as outdoor ones.'

'Did you spend much time with them, growing up?'

'Some,' she said, remembering the way it would make her feel when she would leave home to spend the weekend with her father and then the way it would make her feel to come back home. Awful, awkward and not fitting in at either house. 'I didn't exactly make the best first impression. I was a bit of a wild child, running around naked, making a mess and ruining things. Margaret, Dad's wife, couldn't handle it and, no matter how much I tried to be the kind of daughter she might have in her house, it didn't seem to help.'

'Why bother?' Benoit demanded arrogantly, full of the self-assured confidence she'd never possessed.

'Because I wanted to spend time with my father?' she replied hotly. 'Because I would have liked to have got to know my brother? Because there's half a family out there that is mine and I'm cut off from them? It's not as simple as not caring what other people think, Benoit,' she said, fearing that the tears she felt pressing against the back of her eyes might escape.

She could feel the weight of his gaze on her face, on her skin, warming it, and then it cooled, as if he'd looked away.

'So is that what you'll do with the money?' Benoit asked, purposely changing the subject. They might need to get to know each other, but he didn't want to press any further than he had already. Because there was something about the way she had described being cut off from her family, the hurt there that called to his own, to the way he felt without Xander in his life.

'From the jewels?' she asked, as if needing clarification at the giant shift in conversation. 'No. I think I'm too old to go to university.'

'Oh, I didn't realise that they refused to allow

people to attend university after the age of what, twenty-five?'

'Twenty-six.'

He rolled his eyes. 'So young.'

'And you're positively ancient,' she mocked. 'I wouldn't know what to study,' she said, not quite sure that was true.

He laughed. 'Really? I'd have thought it would be obvious.'

She frowned at him and Benoit wondered that she couldn't see it, how intelligent she was. Her mind was quick and she absorbed information like a sponge. And she was most definitely opinionated. That beat half of the people Chalendar employed and he employed some of the best.

'Sociology or politics. Definitely something to do with gender studies, though you really will have to stop using words like mansplaining and—'

He dodged the pillow she threw at him and laughed while rescuing the glass of wine before it could spill.

'No, university is for Summer. She has the brains; she's applying for her Masters as we speak.'

'And that stops you how?' Benoit asked, unsure as to why she would think any less of herself than her sisters.

'I just…it's not something I'm willing to get into debt over.'

'But we're talking about what happens if you find the jewels. Surely money won't be an issue then and you can spend it on whatever you like.'

'Yes. Of course,' she replied blankly and Benoit had the distinct impression that Skye wouldn't put herself first even if she had all the money in the world. It would go somewhere else, to someone else. And suddenly he was angry with the parents who had made her feel that she was not worthy of wanting such things for herself.

'It's late, so…' she said, unfurling herself from the sofa with an unconscious elegance that drew his gaze. Until she nearly tripped on the hem of his trousers again. She was going to hurt herself in those. He sighed. He'd liked those trousers.

'Come here,' he said, gesturing to her and hauling himself into a more seated position. He patted his pockets for the miniature Swiss army knife on his key chain. In the shadowed room, Skye looked at him with watchful eyes.

He glared up at her and she came close enough for him to snag her hip and pull her in between his legs. He didn't miss the way she flinched, nor the way she had bitten her lip between her teeth as if to stop herself from asking what he was doing. And he was thankful because for a second his mind went blank. He could feel the heat of her cresting over him like the gentlest of waves. His palms itched to feel the back of her thighs, her skin beneath his palm. His pulse jerked and he held his breath so that he couldn't be tantalised by the simple scent of her. No perfume or hair products, or gels or lotions. Just pure Skye.

He made the mistake of looking up. She was watching him, her neck bent so that her hair fell over her face like a waterfall. It reminded him of the plane, of her standing between his legs then, but this was different—*more*, somehow. Large brown eyes with golden flecks watching him, embers flaring, just waiting for a spark to ignite, to burn them both. He heard it, the hitch in her breathing, and warned himself to stop this, but seemed unable to.

He clenched his hand to prevent himself from pulling her towards him and felt the heavy ridged metal shape of the army knife in his palm. He broke the connection of their gaze and knew that he wouldn't look back at her again. Instead, he pulled out the scissor attachment, picked up one loose leg of the trousers at her mid-thigh and snipped.

'What are you—?'

Rip.

The tearing sound cut through the quiet of the room like a scream. He pulled the two edges of the material wide. She started and almost stepped back but, because he still held the material in his hands, couldn't.

'You were going to fall and break something, constantly tripping over the ends of these,' he said, turning his attention to snipping where the material had refused to tear on the inner seem. It had sounded like a growl. Like anger, as if it were her fault his trousers didn't fit her. He had to bend his head to see where to slip the scissors, only he felt a tremor in his hand. And that had nothing to do with anger, but it did have something to do with heat. It was spreading thick and fast over every inch of his skin. Invisible vibrations rattled him. He was always in control, but this? It was testing him.

Finally, he freed the first trouser leg and turned his attention to the other. She took another breath, as if she'd been about to say something, but he focused on the trousers. He felt her relax; the hands that she'd held up at her chest as if to protect herself dropped to her sides and he wished they hadn't. She needed to be on guard around him. She needed to protect herself.

He lined up the shortened leg with the hemline of the second and snipped. Skye's body swayed slightly as he tore the linen, the sound making him think of tearing other clothes from her body, and he made the mistake of looking down at her long shapely legs. The skin so smooth, and barely inches from his mouth, his tongue, his teeth.

'Go to bed,' he commanded without looking up.

She stayed for a moment, as if intending to defy him, but thankfully thought better of it. He sat there for a long time after she went to bed, wrestling with the bindings of the terms he had placed on their agreement.

Skye just didn't know what she was going to find when she came down to breakfast the next day— the charming, at ease playboy or the dark, brooding ruthless magnate. Both felt like an extreme of his personality and she couldn't help but feel that naturally he lay somewhere in the middle. But she was surprised to find him packing a bag when she rounded the corner.

'Going somewhere?' she asked.

'Oui,' he said, tight-lipped.

'Without me?' she asked, instantly wishing she could eat her words.

He paused ever so slightly before pressing a towel into his rucksack. That he'd planned to leave her alone made her feel…something she didn't want to examine too much. But, as much as she didn't like the idea, she wasn't going to force herself even more on a man who'd come here to be completely alone.

'Have fun. I'll...see you when I see you,' she said, cringing as she stuttered over the words that made it clear she didn't want to be left alone.

He sighed and she felt even worse.

'Get yourself a towel,' he threw over his shoulder. Only now she really didn't want to go, but couldn't say so because he'd have to insist that she came and it would be even worse.

Ten minutes later they had left the house and, rather than following the road, they'd cut down a worn path through the rainforest. Unlike before, their footsteps were meandering and the hacking of the machete was not as regular. Bathed in shadows and beams of light, she couldn't stop looking upwards at the way the impossibly tall trees stretched into a canopy high above them. Every single different shade of green she could imagine cocooned them, making her feel oddly safe in this huge expanse. A warmth that was faintly damp and the smell of the rich earth was so very different from the sprawling English forests she was used to. Skye felt alive and present in a way she had never done before.

Benoit looked back at her for a moment, and she wondered what he could see. She knew that the information they'd shared last night had been necessary to fool his family that they were engaged.

Engaged.

The word hit a wall in her mind and fell to the ground with a *thunk*. It still didn't feel real. Neither had last night.

You shouldn't make a gift of yourself like that.

Was that what she'd been doing? Offering herself to Alistair as some kind of thank you for his relationship with her? So desperate for affection or attention because of her parents, so *thankful* that she'd...

Benoit had stopped and she had to pull herself up short to prevent herself from running into the back of him. When she looked up over his shoulder she couldn't help the gasp that fell from her lips. How she'd missed the sound of the stunning waterfall before her she had no idea, until she realised that the dense foliage must have protected them from the gentle roar of the cascade.

A jagged rocky outcrop reached high above them, covered in moss and spindly trees that clung to the stone. Water poured off the edge of the cliff and rushed headlong into a clear blue pool at the base of what must have been a twenty-foot drop. The pool was surrounded by flat rocks, joining the forest floor. It was like something out of a fairy tale.

'It's incredible.'

She felt the heat of his gaze against her cheek, but when she turned to look he was staring at the waterfall.

'I come out here as many times as I can when I'm in Costa Rica. It's so far off the beaten track that only my neighbour and I can access it. But, as we've established, my neighbour is away,' he said, stalking off down the path before she could respond.

'I don't have a swimsuit,' she called after him, mildly frustrated.

'Neither do I,' he growled.

CHAPTER EIGHT

BENOIT HAD STOPPED on a grassy outcrop beside
the pool and dropped his bag. He pulled off his
shirt and toed off his shoes and socks, his fingers
going to his waistband before his hands fisted at
his sides.

She forced air into her lungs as she took in
the powerful shoulders and sculpted chest that
tapered into Benoit's lean hips. Good God, did
people really look like that? Alistair had been a
young tangle of limbs and the majority of the men
working at the construction site had beer bellies
that they joked were 'bought and paid for'. In the
blink of an eye, Benoit dived into the pool, plunging beneath the surface, not emerging until he
was far on the other side, as if he was desperate
to put some distance between them.

He was pushing her away. The realisation hurt,
tapped into deeper issues that she'd long covered
over with roles and duties and responsibilities.
But it also unlocked something within her, be-

cause if he *was* pushing her away then it meant she had come too close. It meant she wasn't the only one feeling…feeling…

She looked back to the other side of the pool, shocked to find Benoit half walking and half climbing up a pathway that she couldn't quite make out. The way the muscles on his back moved, rippling over strong shoulder blades, the powerful width of his arms looking as if he might tear the jagged cliff face down rather than scale it was hypnotic.

By the time he reached the top, Skye had to shield her eyes from the sun and the blush of her cheeks from his gaze because, standing atop the jagged outcrop beside the edge of the waterfall, he looked…like a conqueror—proud, exhilarated. And for just a moment she saw it—*felt* it—the entire weight of his gaze, his focus, his attention bearing down on her like a physical thing. Her heart stopped, her breath caught in her lungs, and then he soared into the air, his perfect dive slicing into the crystal blue pool below. It was over in a matter of seconds, but her quick mind had captured every detail, every movement his body made, her ears barely hearing the break of the water beneath him.

She didn't release her breath until he emerged from the water, shaking dark golden tendrils of hair from his face, sending droplets scattering across the surface of the pool. His mouth was still a thin line, but his eyes…they were electric. Zipping and zapping sparks of adrenaline and excitement that were so tempting.

'Your turn,' he said. He didn't have to shout, to project his voice. She heard it as clearly as if he were standing next to her.

'I don't think so,' she replied, only the words felt like a lie on her tongue.

He stayed where he was in the pool, just staring at her, holding his gaze on her as if he could tell, as if he knew that she wanted to take that leap as much as she needed her next breath.

'I have no intention of repeating myself,' he warned.

Skye looked up at the waterfall, the pathway that Benoit had made look easy, and she wanted it. Wanted to know what he'd felt, what he'd experienced that had made him look so *alive*. The yearning in her stomach reminded her of how she had felt last night, standing between his legs, so close to him. The thrill, the fear, the excitement rippling from her core outwards over her body.

An ache formed in her chest, one of pure want, like nothing she'd ever experienced before. As if she were building towards something that only leaping from the top of the waterfall could satisfy.

Without another word, she pulled her shirt over her head and Benoit turned away as if it had nothing to do with her modesty and more to do with a lack of interest. And it stung. It stung because she couldn't deny how much she wanted him any more. But the hurt didn't stop the aching need; it simply made it more obvious.

She kicked off her shoes and the shorts, ignoring the embarrassment she felt about being in her soon-to-be wet underwear. She dived into the water and reached the other side before she could change her mind. She dragged herself out onto the rocky outcrop, where Benoit was already standing. He barely looked at her and it only made her more determined.

'Follow where I put my feet and hands.'

She didn't bother replying. If he was going to be a monosyllabic brute then so be it.

She had expected the climb to be much harder, to hurt her feet, but the stone had been worn away by years and years of people doing exactly what they were about to do. As they got higher, the roar of the water was deafening and the spray flicked against her skin, making her feel hyperaware.

They reached the top and for a second the sudden absence of sound and spray was disorientating, but not as much as the view. The pool at the bottom looked a million miles away and she backed away from the edge, right into Benoit's chest.

The adrenaline in her body turned to fear, her

legs trembled and her stomach twisted. She'd
been wrong; she couldn't do this. She suddenly
wanted to go home. Not back to his house or the
estate in Norfolk, but to her little house in the
New Forest. To life before Costa Rica, Benoit and
the search for the jewels. She wanted to live in
the bubble that she'd been happy with until she'd
exposed her life to Benoit and found it wanting.

His hand was on her shoulder, steadying her
but also keeping her literally at arm's length.

'I can't do this,' she said, the trembling in her
legs getting worse.

'Why not?'

'It's not who I am. I don't do this kind of thing,'
she said, leaning forward a little to peer down at
the pool below and wondering how difficult it
would be to climb back down. Gently, he pulled
her back and turned her to face him. The way his
eyes bored into hers, the icy blue depths glinting not with charm but determination struck her
to her core.

'I don't want you to be something you're not.
I want you to embrace who you are.'

Skye had to work so hard to keep the sob that
rose in her chest from escaping. It felt as if in
three days Benoit had unearthed the cornerstone
of her entire being and it hurt. It hurt because she
knew that he was right. That she needed to heal
that part of herself that was always trying to be

whatever other people needed her to be and not what she needed for herself.

'What do you see when you look at me?' she asked, unable to prevent the question falling from her lips and unwilling to meet his eyes.

'That's the point, Skye. It's not about what *I* see, but what *you* see.'

And with that he stepped past her and jumped, soaring into the sky and over the edge of the waterfall. Skye counted the rapid heartbeats fluttering in her chest until she heard the splash of water and knew that he was safe.

She expected her pulse to slow, but it didn't. Because it was her turn. She knew she could climb back down. After all, it was up to her and that was just as much a part of the point he was making. But she didn't want to. She remembered the thrill in his eyes just after he'd jumped the first time, the excitement stirring in her own body, the desire to feel that for herself. She approached the area where Benoit had jumped from. What was the worst that could happen? She could fall and break her heart. Arm, she corrected; she'd meant arm, obviously.

Before she could change her mind, she bent her legs and launched herself away from the grassy bank at the edge of the waterfall, shaping her body into a dive. It was as if everything she felt rushed through her in less than a second. Fear, happiness, excitement, pleasure. She was pretty sure she screamed, but by the time she rose from the depths of the water below she knew one thing about herself for certain.

She was someone who jumped off waterfalls and loved it.

Now she wanted to know what would happen if she took a different kind of leap.

Benoit let the spray from the shower clean away the sweat and traces of dirt from the return journey through the rainforest. It pummelled his skin but it wasn't enough. He switched the temperature to cold, then freezing. Anything to shock his system into clearing the kaleidoscope of erotic images of Skye from his mind. Skye in her wet underwear, climbing up the side of the waterfall like a sprite, emerging from the water and sweeping her hair from her face, her strong legs and arms holding her steady in the water.

Just like he'd dreamed the night before. At first his dreams had been intense and mouth-wateringly erotic; he could have slept for ever with dreams like that. But then, just before dawn, they'd changed. In his bedroom, in his *bed*, he'd found Skye in a red negligee with a faceless man and he'd woken with his heart pounding and a cold sweat over his entire body.

Was it a warning? Not about Skye—he didn't

think for a second she would do such a thing. But for himself. He, of all people, knew that his judgement was unsound around women. Camilla, his mother—he should never forget that. So that morning he'd planned to go to the waterfall alone to get his head straight. But the way she'd looked at him at breakfast… And then, at the waterfall, the diamonds in her eyes after she'd jumped… It was as if he felt what she did—the adrenaline rush, that power. She'd jumped the very first time. Her strength was something he'd never questioned about her, but she seemed not to realise it about herself and that was a tragedy.

It had been getting dark by the time they'd returned to the house and now the patio was lit by the moon and stars overhead. He wrapped a towel around his waist and stalked back into the house, feeling angry. Angry at Skye, angry at himself. No, he corrected, not one for self-deceit, it wasn't anger—it was frustration. He wanted Skye with an intensity that he'd not experienced before, even with Camilla. And he had been stupid enough to make a deal that involved keeping her in his life for another three years. Once they were married he'd let her return to England. He simply couldn't be this close to temptation all the time. Because he was certain that he would destroy her. As he'd nearly destroyed his brother the night his mother had left.

He walked through the house and up the stairs, seeing no sign of Skye as he made his way to the bedroom. But he couldn't shake the feeling that she hadn't gone to bed. In his room, he threw the towel into the basket in the corner and pulled on a pair of loose black cotton trousers, the material for the first time awkward against his skin. Something was tearing at his insides to get out, something he'd not wanted to face for years.

The door to his room opened, drawing his gaze from the window to where Skye stood outlined in a halo of light. He ground his teeth together. She was wearing his shirt. Nothing else. The image was seared into his brain in the time it took to realise that Skye was unaware of what the light behind her revealed. He could see the shape of her hips against the thin linen material, the dip of her waist, the slight shadow of the curve of her breast and the seemingly endless expanse of the smooth pale skin of her thighs.

He clenched his hand to stop himself from reaching for her.

'You haven't spoken a word to me since we left the waterfall.'

'And you think coming here, now, you'll find what you're looking for?'

'Yes.'

He turned his back on her, on the temptation that she presented, and looked out across the dark shadow of forest beyond the windows. He shouldn't have pushed her at the waterfall. He just… He'd just wanted her to know. How amazing she could be if she stopped letting other people dictate who she was.

He heard her take another step into the room and closed his eyes. This could ruin everything. They had a perfect deal. Each would get what they wanted and walk away.

'Why do you cut yourself off from everything here?' she asked, her English accent so clear and unwavering.

It wasn't the question he'd been expecting so it took him a moment to shift mental gears. A moment in which she took another step forward. He felt it.

'Because it's completely cut off from the rest of my life.'

She nodded as if she not only understood but had expected the answer. 'It's contained.'

He frowned, but yes—it was contained.

'As if,' she said, coming another step towards him, 'what happens here doesn't affect what happens there.'

He stilled, realising where she was going with this but not sure he wanted to follow.

'Does it work the other way round?' she asked, and her simple question raised the hairs on his forearms. She was asking too much.

'No one else has ever been here to find out,' he said. He was losing the fight because he wanted something in his mouth other than the taste of guilt and regret. He wanted her.

Skye stood by his side and as she looked out through the window she let him study her, take her in; she felt his gaze against her skin, where his eyes roamed across her face and back.

'We have a deal,' he snarled, not scaring her in the least. She knew he was struggling with this. Knew that he wanted her as much as she wanted him. 'You've agreed to be my wife—for three years. If this gets—'

'You think because I'm inexperienced I won't be able to separate this night from our deal? Or do you think because I'm a woman I won't be able to separate my emotions from—?'

'It's not you,' he growled. 'It's me. It's me because I know, deep down, I am my parents' child—selfish and always one step away from doing whatever the hell I want. And, believe me, I want you. But it can't happen.'

He finally turned to face her and the look in his eyes stole her breath. She could see he was fighting it and it made her angry.

'Really? You spent all day pushing me, probing my emotions and hurts, demanding that I accept myself just as I am. You tell me to go for what I want and then tell me I can't have it?'

His eyes flared in the dark room, the moon shooting stars across his icy blue irises.

'One night? You just want one night?'

'Yes,' she breathed, not caring about the longing in her voice.

'It will never be enough, Skye.'

'Your arrogance is astounding,' she breathed, outraged.

'I didn't mean for you.' His voice was dark, angry with warning. It matched the fire he'd started within her and there was only one way forward now—to let it burn.

'It will have to be,' she said on a shaky breath. Because she wasn't ready for more. She wasn't sure she'd ever be ready for more.

She looked up at him to see if he'd heard, or even understood. He watched her for so long she was ready to turn and leave, when finally he nodded. Once.

And that was all the warning she had before his lips crashed down on hers, his hands coming to frame her face, pressing against her hair and anchoring her to him, angling her to him in a way that she couldn't resist. She opened up for him, his tongue plunging deep within her, filling her in a way that she felt she'd missed her entire life.

Her hands flew to his shoulders, holding on

as he feasted upon her, but also taking something for herself. His smooth, hot skin was perfect beneath her palms, her fingers flying over his collarbone to the stretch of his powerful traps, around his shoulders and down his sides. She felt like a sculptress, learning the figure she wanted to create by touch.

Each inch of skin she discovered was incredible but not enough. *More, more, more.* It was like a mantra turning over again and again in her mind. She wanted absolutely everything he could give her. He walked her back a step and she felt the coolness of the glass at her back through the thin linen shirt covering her fevered skin. He left her lips swollen and ravished as he bent his mouth to her neck, pressing open-mouthed kisses beneath her jawline down to her shoulder, where he gently bit down on her flesh. Her core clenched in reaction, desire and heat pooling low and throbbing.

Unable to help herself, she arched her chest to his, needing to feel him against her body. Benoit threaded an arm behind her in the space she had created, hauling her against him, and she lifted her leg, shamelessly hooking it around his hip and pressing into his erection.

The feel of it, of him, between her legs was indescribable. Her head fell back in pleasure as he continued to kiss, suck, lick, bite his way across her shoulder. His free arm came up in between them, his hand angling her head back so that he could lavish attention on her body. His fingers traced downwards, finding the central notch with his index finger, then her sternum, following the motion with his tongue until he veered off as his fingers found one nipple and his mouth the other.

She cried out. She couldn't help it. Never had she felt so utterly devoured and sure. Sure that there was even more pleasure to be had. An impatience was building within her, a need that she couldn't control. She curved into the hardness of his arousal and he growled against her breast, clenching the hand now fisting her bottom.

Nothing. She'd felt *nothing* like this before. Thoughts flitted through her mind at lightning speed. Benoit's dark glare…showering outside in the garden…swimming in the pool beneath the waterfall… Benoit hauling himself out onto the rocky outcrop…

You don't behave as if someone has given you pleasure.

Standing between his legs as he tore the linen trousers…

I want you to embrace who you are.

Jumping off the cliff…

Each thought merged with the way he touched her, the way he pulled desire and cries of pleasure from her soul. He pursed his lips around her nipple and she bucked away from the pleasure, pressing back against the glass. At the release of her breast she looked up and met eyes that were glistening like freshly formed frost beneath the moon. Intent, dark and devastating, he didn't take his eyes from her once as he tore at the button of the shorts and thrust them down her thighs. He was daring her, challenging her to stop him.

In that moment she knew she never would.

Still without taking his eyes from hers, he hooked his thumb beneath the waistband of her briefs, giving her a chance to stop him every step of the way. The power that hummed beneath her skin, the complete assurance that she was in control, that she could stop this at any point, the knowledge that he would stop, was intoxicating.

He seemed angry that she didn't. A look of resignation crossed his features for a second before desire blotted out everything and, finally, he broke their gaze as he turned his attention to where his thumb was pulling down the thin material of her briefs.

Benoit cursed. He cursed himself, cursed her, and cursed the fact that she looked, smelt, felt, tasted like everything he'd ever wanted. Slowly, inch by inch, he removed her panties, teasing her, teasing himself, he just didn't know any more.

You don't behave as if someone has given you pleasure.

He wished he'd never said it to her, because now it was all he could think of—giving her so much pleasure it overflowed. The delicate cross-hatching of curls at the apex of her legs was perfect to him and he anchored his hands at her hips, coming down onto his knees. She wriggled in his grasp and he couldn't help the spike of pleasure that flared, knowing that she was just as affected by this as he was—affected, tested, delighted. There were such fine lines between the range of feelings surging through him.

He brought his hands down around the curve of her bottom, cupping and tilting her pelvis, causing her legs to splay slightly—enough. Enough for him to bend his head, to press his mouth to her core. He ran his tongue the entire length of her, loving the way she parted for him, thrilled by the taste of her, delighted by the sobs of sheer pleasure that fell from her mouth into the air about them.

He found the soft nub of her clitoris and she trembled in his hands, her pleasure heightening his to an ache, throbbing and hardening and roaring for release. The shakes cascading through her body edged her closer and then further from his mouth. And it wasn't enough. He wanted her completely at his mercy, just as he felt at hers.

He released one hand from the back of her thigh, bringing it round to lift just behind her knee and place it over his shoulder, giving him greater access. His tongue fastened against her clitoris, he pressed a finger to her core and heard the sound of her back hitting the glass; faster and faster he heard her inhale, filling her lungs with air as he continued to fill her with his hands and mouth.

Until that moment—the moment where everything stopped...breath, thought, heartbeat...and he felt her come apart against his fingers and tongue. He consumed it all, everything she had to give and more. He held her through it all.

When the trembling in her body finally stopped, he picked her up and took her to the bed, laying her gently down on the mattress, her skin flushed and eyes closed.

'You were right,' she whispered. He wouldn't do her the disservice of asking what she meant. He knew. No one had given her pleasure before.

He stayed at the end of the bed, looking down on her. No matter how much he wanted to move, to lean over her, to touch her everywhere, to taste, to fill her completely, he wouldn't move until he was completely sure.

'We can stop now,' he said, even though he knew what her answer would be.

'More.'

'What?' He wasn't sure he'd heard the word that had escaped her mouth; her eyes were still closed in bliss.

She slowly opened them, leant back on her elbows, levelled him with a stare and said, 'More.' Her voice was strong and clear, her cheeks were flushed; he could tell that it took a lot for her to say it, but he knew she meant it.

Skye watched him climb onto the bed, over her, surrounding her completely, with an anticipation that rivalled any she'd ever experienced. Her heart was still beating a wild tattoo from an orgasm that had felt as if it had been trapped within her for years. Benoit came so far up the bed she had to crane her neck to look back at him, arching her back, feeling utterly surrounded by him. He smiled down at her, but it was one of pure wickedness and she loved it.

He leaned back on his haunches, bringing his lips to hers and kissed her like she'd never been kissed before. It wasn't forceful, desperate or even lazy; it was…consuming. Her hands went to his head, to hold him there, but he reached for them and pushed them above her head, holding them there with his free hand while the other trailed an open palm down her neck, sternum and over her breast.

'If you keep touching me, Skye, I won't last,'

he said but, rather than sounding weak, it only made her feel strong. She moaned into his mouth and he took it. He took everything.

His hand dipped lower, around her hip and to her inner thigh, gently moving it so that he could come between them. He broke the kiss and locked his eyes with hers. There was no challenge this time, no warning, no anger. This time she felt... assurance. Once again he was giving her power, only this time it felt as if he were trusting her with it.

He entered her slowly and she gasped for air as the length and width of him gently pushed at her muscles, filling her bit by bit but so completely. He never broke eye contact the entire time. Her eyes drifted closed as she got used to the incredible feeling of him within her. And when he pushed further, closer to that indefinable place that she both craved and wanted to delay, her eyes burst open to see him watching her in wonder.

He hadn't been talking about an orgasm, she realised—what Benoit had said about pleasure. It wasn't about an end goal, some point to achieve, but the feeling of luxuriating in ongoing pleasure—*that* was what he'd been talking about and *that* was what he was doing now. Unfurling a seemingly endless wave of pleasure and delight, filling her, overwhelming her, building within her until it poured over and out of her.

For what felt like hours Benoit moved within her, slowly, deeply, incredibly. Sweat slicked their bodies, the air was heated with cries and moans of delight, building a fire within them both. Her hand slid down the side of his body, around the curve of his ass, his hip, and a thread of excitement lit within her as she found where they were joined together.

Her only warning was his growl and then all she could do was hold on in utter glory as he thrust into her again and again, deeper, faster, harder, and her mind could barely register the pleasure that was raining down over her. Her panting met his growls, her fingers flew to his shoulders and her nails dug into his skin; his grip on her hips became an anchor until her breathing began to stutter as she got closer and closer...

'Skye—'

'Oh, God.' She couldn't help the words falling from her mouth. Encouragements, pleas, demands, threats...all were uttered as he drove them off a cliff face into bliss.

CHAPTER NINE

THUD, THUD, THUD, THUD...

At first Skye thought the sound was coming from her body, her heartbeat still erratic from her night with Benoit. But when she lifted herself onto her hands, his plush mattress cushioning her wrists, she realised it was something else. She was about to ask Benoit what was going on when she saw the door to his bedroom swing closed.

The rhythmic sound continued for a little longer before slowing to a stop. The sun had risen and soft beams of light were filtered through the thick foliage outside the windows.

She sat and turned, bringing the high thread count sheets to her chest, the motion making her aware of a pleasurable ache between her legs and she felt...amazing. A flush rose to her cheeks at the memory of what they had shared the night before—the way Benoit had held her as she had come apart in his arms more than once. Even thinking of it brought echoes of the pleasure she had experienced and she fisted her hands against the memories.

One night... It will never be enough.

She had been so sure of herself when she'd only had Alistair as a reference. But now she knew. She knew better. He'd been right. One night was not enough.

Benoit pushed into the room, the door bouncing back against the wall, and she sat further up in the bed.

'What's going on?' she asked, shocked at the sudden transformation.

'The helicopter. It's here. Apparently someone found the car, contacted the police, who alerted my great-aunt. I have to—' He stopped himself. Took a breath. '*We* are going back to France. Now.'

The helicopter ride was incredible. Much like the jump from the waterfall, it was over in what seemed like even half a second and she couldn't shake the feeling that she was hurtling towards an ending she wasn't prepared for. Even though, surely, if she was marrying Benoit then she had another three years? But the speed with which she found herself being led up the ramp of a private plane at Limón Airport made her feel slightly nauseous.

She frowned as she saw Benoit handing over a

key. It was the key for the locker where she had left her bags and, more importantly, her phone charger. Her sisters. The map. She was horrified that she'd almost forgotten them.

A flight attendant, picture perfect with bright red lipstick and an immaculately clean pressed uniform, asked if she would like a drink. Skye shook her head, feeling completely out of her depth. She must have looked a fright in torn linen shorts and a clearly Benoit-sized white shirt. She was led to a seat she was afraid to use in case her clothes were too dirty or that she would damage it. She had known that Benoit was rich, but this? She shook her head.

'Ça va?' he asked.

She leaned her head to one side, not quite sure how to answer the question.

'My clothes; they're…'

'You're worried about your clothes?' he asked as if he too was finally considering all the things that they *did* have to worry about.

A gentle laugh fell from her lips. 'I'm not sure that even my luggage contains clothing suitable for…' *what is about to happen*, she finished silently. She wasn't sure *she* was suitable for what was about to happen.

'I'll arrange for you to have suitable clothes upon arrival in France.'

'You know my size?' Skye instantly regretted

the way her voice squeaked at an unreasonably high pitch on the last word.

He simply looked at her. The old arrogant, monosyllabic Benoit was back, but this time she saw memories of last night dance across the icy blue depths.

Benoit went to check in with the pilot and complete the necessary paperwork, and all Skye was left with was a sense of foreboding. As if soon being able to turn on her phone had conjured the fear that something awful had happened, that her sisters had been trying desperately to contact her, that everything had gone wrong in her absence. So by the time Benoit's assistant rolled her luggage along the jet's small gangway she was ready to burst.

'*Mademoiselle?*' he offered.

'*Merci, merci.*' She batted the small man aside and dragged the case onto the table in front of her, unzipped the hardened top and thrust in a hand to retrieve her charger. She plugged it into the socket she had already identified and scrabbled for her phone in her handbag. She probably looked like a madwoman but Skye didn't care. She had to wait another infuriating two minutes while her completely dead phone registered enough charge to turn on, but finally the flashing green battery image appeared and it sprang to life in her hands. She quickly turned down the volume, expecting

a barrage of twenty or more beeps from a series
of increasingly worried messages from her sisters... But there was nothing.

She checked the socket, and the input port for
the cable. Frowning, she turned her attention back
to the screen as it vibrated just once.

Hey sis, hope you're having FUN! :) Have sent you
an email with latest journal info and relevant sec-
tions. Catherine travelled to Arabia! After scan-
dalous rel with Benoit forced her out of England.
Long story! All in email. Love S&S

And that was it.

Skye had disappeared from the face of the
planet for more than three days. And nothing.
Her sisters hadn't worried—hadn't contacted the
British Embassy, the coastguard or anyone else.
They'd hoped she was *having fun.*

She fell back against the seat and stared out of
the window. It hurt, she realised. Hurt that they
hadn't worried about her in the same way that she
worried about them. Guilt sliced through her. Of
course she hadn't wanted anything bad to have
happened to them, but...but it was clear that they
didn't need her. All this time, for as long as she
could remember, that was what had driven her—
the conviction that without her they wouldn't be
okay. She had made almost her entire life about

them and she couldn't blame them for not having the same focus on her, because that was what she'd intended when she'd decided to step up to the role that her mother had stood back from. She'd *wanted* them to have their lives and live them. But...

'Are you not going to call them?' Benoit asked from where he stood at the top of the walkway in front of the cockpit.

Skye forced a smile to her lips. 'We're so close to finding the map, I thought I'd wait until I know where I...where *we* stand.'

Instead, fighting back the sting of tears, she fired off a text.

Lots of fun. Will tell you all about it soon. Just off to France (!) to see if the map is still with the Chalendars. Will take a look at email asap. Love S

Given just how desperately she had tried to escape in Costa Rica, Benoit was a little surprised that Skye had barely touched her phone. He couldn't take his eyes off her as she put her phone down and looked out of the window. His fiancée...

A fiancée he'd spent the entire night before thoroughly ravishing. In an instant he was hard and was forced to pull his laptop closer so as not to embarrass the flight attendant. He took a deep breath to calm himself, deeply resentful of the way even just the thought of her raised his pulse and blood pressure. He was thankful that she'd had the presence of mind to insist on only one night. Because even just one more night and Benoit was almost one hundred per cent sure that he'd never be able to let her go, let alone out of his bed. Never had he experienced anything like it. In the past, his tastes had been wide, varied and thoroughly investigated. But Skye...seeing her fall apart, feeling it in his hands, against his mouth...

He cursed out loud, drawing a frown from Skye before she resumed her watchful gaze at the window. He needed the flight back to the Dordogne to get himself under control. Because if he didn't he could lose everything.

Just over eleven hours later the jet taxied on the small private landing strip near the chateau in the Dordogne. He'd spent the entire flight furiously countering demands, threats and coercive emails from the family board members about the upcoming meeting in two days, tight-lipped and grim-faced while Skye slept and drifted to her phone during her waking moments, reading, frowning, smiling...her face so expressive as she reacted to whatever she was reading.

As the jet finally came to a stop, he stood and

walked over to where Skye was, once again, asleep. Just before rousing her, he saw the petite frame of his great-aunt through the small circular window, swathed in layers of silk tugged about her on the wind, holding an impossibly tiny creature in her arms. He bit back a curse. The chihuahua had hated him on first sight and ever since had made numerous attempts to destroy any kind of footwear he possessed.

'Benoit?'

He looked down at Skye, who was slowly blinking her eyes open in a way that he'd missed that morning in Costa Rica before the helicopter arrived. He felt an urge to smile, to soften the edge of concern he saw in her gaze—which was precisely why he didn't. 'We're here.'

'The map,' she exclaimed eagerly.

He was thankful that at least one of them had some last thread of common sense.

'We have a welcoming party.' He gestured to where Skye would be able to see Anaïs through the window, hoping that she was ready. Because he sure as hell wasn't.

The wind that whipped about her took Skye by surprise. But not as much as the look on the older woman's face the moment she locked gazes with Skye. A sharp, high pitched *yap* drew Skye's attention to Anaïs' folded arms where something struggled within the swathes of pink and cream silk covering the woman's diminutive frame. With a sigh, Anaïs bent to the floor and released a tiny dog, straining at its lead as if the small animal was determined to break free and ravage... Benoit? Yes. Most definitely the chihuahua's focus was fixed on the man behind her on the steps leading down from the small jet.

Clearly, he and the little dog had history. But when Skye's gaze met with Anaïs, once again she felt an unusual sense that the woman was pleased to see her. There was an unaccountable look of recognition in her eyes but Skye wasn't quite sure how that could possibly be.

'Benoit Chalendar, the first thing you are going to do is get rid of that beard,' Anaïs said in English as he hugged her, her hand reaching for the jawline Skye now knew intimately.

'It is lovely to see you too, Anaïs,' he said, leaning into her hand and pressing a kiss into the palm. 'I am well, thank you for asking,' he said, somehow managing to dodge the chihuahua without inflicting damage on the small dog trying to devour his leather shoes. When Anaïs bent to pick up the yapping dog, Skye was sure she heard Benoit chide her for encouraging 'the little beast'.

'And your hair needs a trim. You look like a

hippy,' Anaïs stated firmly whilst managing to convey a heart full of love within the words.

Benoit cast a look to Skye before replying. 'I promise to address the situation, once we've had refreshments and time to catch up.'

Anaïs followed Benoit's look and nodded. 'In the library, I think.'

'We don't usually meet in the library.' Benoit frowned.

'This time we will,' she said assuredly, leaning past Benoit and holding out an exquisitely jewelled hand. 'Anaïs Chalendar. It is nice to finally meet you.'

As Anaïs led them back through the jaw-dropping grounds of a chateau that looked as if it had come straight out of the fairy tales she used to read to Summer and Star when they were young, Skye turned over Anaïs' words in her mind, trying to make them fit. *Finally?* Did Anaïs already know that she was to marry her great-nephew?

Finding no sensible answer, Skye turned her attention to the surroundings. The chateau was beautiful and in a way, cast in the soft setting sun, it seemed everything that the dark, downtrodden Soames estate in Norfolk was not. Gorgeous light blond-coloured stones made up the brickwork of the large two-storey chateau. Little balconies wrapped around tall double-fronted windows, some of which were open, and glimpses of expensive curtains billowing in the breeze made the building feel lived-in and welcoming.

But Anaïs, despite her small stature and what must have been considerable age, was leading them along at a brisk clip. It might have been less ostentatious than the Soames estate, but this building felt more welcoming and loved. As Anaïs led them into the cooler, darker interior, Skye barely had time to take note of the hallways and corridors she found herself in.

'You grew up here?' she asked Benoit in awe.

He nodded. 'My father and mother had the east wing, and after he died...well, Anaïs moved us to the west wing, nearer to her living quarters.'

It was imposing and impossibly grand, but every now and then she thought she could see traces of similarities to the Soames estate. Neither, of course, was anything like the little house that she, her sisters and her mother had shared when they were younger.

Anaïs held the door to the library open and the moment that Skye stepped into the room the air whooshed from her lungs on a sudden, *'Oh!'*

Skye turned to see a large smile across Anaïs' lovely features.

'I thought as much,' the older woman said with a satisfied nod.

'Thought what? Anaïs, what is going on?' Benoit asked from behind Skye, clearly out of the loop of the unspoken back and forth between her and Skye.

It was an exact replica of the library at the Soames estate. There were slight differences in the décor, but essentially it was the same layout. Skye's eyes flew to the window on the left-hand side and she didn't need to go into the hallway to know that the room was the same mis-sized shape as Catherine's library.

'Ms Soames, I have been waiting quite some time to meet you,' Anaïs said, holding out her hand. Skye took the warm delicate hand in her own, channelling as much of her emotions as she could into the simple gesture. 'I believe you know where to find it?' the older woman said with a smile.

'May I?' she asked, permission the only thing holding her back.

'Of course.'

'What is going on?' Skye heard Benoit demand as she went to the shelves to find the hidden release she knew would be there. As Skye retrieved the package contained in the recess, Anaïs began her story.

'Years ago, my grandfather, Benoit, entrusted me with a secret, a responsibility that I have had for nearly my entire life. He told me about Catherine and their relationship in England,' she said, smiling towards Skye, 'always ensuring that I knew he loved his wife and children. But Catherine had been his first love. She had written to him just before her marriage to her cousin and explained that she needed him to keep the map a secret. That one day someone from her lineage would come looking for it and that he was the only person she trusted to keep the map of the secret passageways and rooms of her English estate safe. She swore to burn her copy and leave the rest to fate.'

'But how did you know that was Skye?' Benoit asked.

'My dear boy, do you really think I would just sit around and wait for some stranger to turn up? You're not the only one able to hire a private investigator, you know.'

Thankfully, his great-aunt turned back to Skye before she could see or hear him choking on his tea.

'You're the oldest, are you not?'

'Yes, Madame Chalendar.'

'Mademoiselle,' Anaïs corrected. 'I traced your mother to the south of England and when I discovered that she had three daughters I hoped that you might be the ones to finally follow the path that Catherine laid out all those years ago.'

Benoit frowned, the suspicion growing that *this* was the family duty that Anaïs had often referred to throughout his childhood—not the family business—shaking him to his core.

'Had not Ms Soames arrived within my lifetime, then I would have passed the responsibility to you,' she said to him.

Benoit was distracted from further thought as Skye took a seat beside his great-aunt with the cloth bundle in her lap. Fingers trembling, she reached for the strings that bound the package and began to release the contents.

There was a thickly bound old-fashioned map which could only have been the plans for her grandfather's estate, something that looked like a letter bearing the name Soames in strong handwriting and a ring. He watched as she held it up to the light, three citrine stones sparkling and set within a gold band.

'Is that one of the Soames jewels?' Benoit asked.

'*Non, chéri*. My grandfather gave Catherine this ring, but she returned it with the map and letter,' Anaïs explained. It was beautiful and he was surprised to see Skye so easily discard it. Instead, she turned her attention to the map and began to unfold it. It looked ancient, the paper having aged into a beautiful golden colour over the hundred plus years it had remained hidden. The map was a study in fine detail, clearly outlining the design of a sprawling estate with secondary passages and chambers within the walls.

'There are so many of them. Surely they can't all be intact?'

'It would take a long time to search them all,' Benoit realised.

'Time we don't have. The will stipulates only two months before the entire estate is given over to the National Trust.'

Benoit watched as Skye snapped a few pictures of the map with her phone, then she was lost in attaching them to a message to her sisters.

Both Benoit and Anaïs were quiet as she did so, but he couldn't shake the watchful eyes of his great-aunt. There was something she wasn't telling him. But whether that was connected with Skye or not he couldn't quite tell.

'My sister emailed me transcriptions of Catherine's journals. I wondered if you might like to read them,' Skye asked Anaïs.

The older woman's face melted into a smile. 'I'd like that very much. I only had Benoit's part of the story all these years and have often wondered about Catherine.'

'I think she loved him greatly, even though she knew it would never be possible for them to be together.'

Anaïs patted Skye's hand. 'Now, my dear, I'm sorry to ask, but there are a few things I need to discuss with my great-nephew. Perhaps you would like to freshen up? I'll have someone show you to a room.'

Benoit registered Skye's response and intention to update her sisters despite the discomfort that had entered his chest.

'"We have a duty to the past. A responsibility to bear for future generations to come." I always thought you meant Chalendar Enterprises, but *this* is what you really meant, isn't it?' he said when Skye had left.

'Yes, I'm sorry that you misunderstood,' Anaïs replied, the pity in her eyes too much.

'You've kept secrets,' he accused.

'As have you. What's going on with the girl?'

'She's not a girl, Anaïs. She's my fiancée.'

Benoit tried to hold her gaze as it felt as if Anaïs peered into his soul. He fought the anger in him that cried that she had forced this on him. That the board would have given up the by-law without her interference.

'Are you sure? She seems like a lovely young woman.'

'She is and I am.' He couldn't quite understand why Anaïs seemed a little sad. Surely this was what she wanted? Disappointment hung heavily in the air between them.

'This is what you wanted, isn't it?' he demanded.

'Not like this,' she said, cupping his jaw with her delicate hand.

'I'm not like him,' he said to himself as much as her.

'In so many wonderful ways you are not like him, *mon coeur.*'

'Then why?' he asked, his voice barely above a whisper, not quite sure he was ready to hear the answer.

'Because I do not have many years left and when I'm gone I don't want the company to be all you have left. And that *would be* like your father. He cut himself off emotionally from everyone and I don't like to see you do the same.'

Something cracked in Benoit's chest—a tendril of grief and loneliness bleeding out at the thought of it.

'But actually,' Anaïs pressed on in a voice stronger and more determined than a woman half her age, 'I wanted to talk to you about another matter. Xander is coming to the family gathering tomorrow and you should know that he has filed for divorce from Camilla.'

Benoit spent an hour walking around the grounds of the chateau with a bottle of whisky as his only companion. He'd failed to notice how the sky had darkened into night, how the seconds had slipped into minutes, which had crept towards an hour.

He knew that he should get back to Skye, but couldn't quite bring himself to do so yet.

Too much was swirling around in his mind. That he'd taken on the mantle of the company because he'd misunderstood Anaïs' cryptic words about duty to the past. That she had forced the vote on the board because she wanted more than the company for him? And more, the argument he'd had with her about Xander still rang in his ears. The first thought he'd had—and had the misfortune to voice—was to wonder whether Xander's divorce would rule him out of the running for CEO.

Enough, Anaïs had commanded. *When did you start to lose your human decency?*

Camilla is a viper, he'd replied.

Yes, one who chose to bite Xander instead of you—and have you given no thought to the effects of the poison?

No, he hadn't. For two years Benoit had refused to allow his thoughts to settle anywhere near his brother and his ex-girlfriend. He was well practised in shifting his mind away from the painful betrayal and now, when he might have wanted to look slightly closer at it, his mind would still not allow it.

Unthinking, his feet had turned in the direction of the chateau, had led him down hallways and up staircases that led to the room he knew his great-aunt had put Skye in. The entire time, the small object in his pocket had found its way into his palm, then onto the tip of his finger. He pulled his hand from his pocket now to knock on the door, inexplicably desperate to see her, unbelievably hopeful that somehow she'd soothe the raging beast within him.

When he heard no answer Benoit turned the handle and opened the door, but his mind couldn't quite work out what he was seeing. Skye's travel case was on the bed but, rather than her taking clothes out of it, she seemed to be in the middle of putting them back in. The rage he'd only just managed to suppress built within him.

'What are you doing?'

Skye looked up, shocked to see him standing in the doorway, filling it completely. She wanted to curse, to scream and cry out. She hadn't wanted him to catch her running away. She hadn't even wanted to run away. Not really. She had given him her word and that meant something to her. But her sisters came first. They always did and they always would.

The moment she'd got to the room, excitement coursing through her veins at finally having found the map, she couldn't wait to speak to her sisters. It was as if she'd jumped from the top of the waterfall all over again. She'd called them instantly and Summer had been just as excited, squealing in delight.

But when Skye had asked about Star, Summer had gone very quiet...

'It's not what you think. I came back to my room and called my sisters and... I can't stay,' she said. 'I *have* to go. Star has run off to some desert kingdom in the Middle East, chasing down the key to the room where the jewels are hidden, and she's just not equipped to handle that. She's too innocent, naïve. I can't let her...' There were no words left. She couldn't put them up fast enough as a barrier between herself and the man staring at her with an intensity and emotion she didn't want to name. 'It's only for a few days.'

'Really? A few days? Come on, Skye,' he said as if he really wondered whether she was lying to herself as much as him. Perhaps she was. 'Once you're there you'll find a way to convince yourself that your sisters need your help, that they're unable to do what needs to be done. Because for some reason you don't think that they're capable of coping without you. You're going to rush back to England so that you can...what? Fly off to the Middle East instead of Star? Arrange for the sale of the house instead of Summer?'

Every single one of his words hurt, sliced into the thin excuses she had drawn about herself like a cloak.

'No! I just need to find out what's going on. And then I'll come back,' she said, her voice weak to her own ears.

'We both know that's a lie.'

He let the accusation stand between them and finally she tossed the shirt she had gripped and scrunched in her hands into the travel case.

'Were you even going to say goodbye?' he demanded.

'Of course I was,' Skye replied, barely managing to choke past the lie that fell so easily from her lips.

'There's no *of course* about it. My mother didn't.'

CHAPTER TEN

THERE WAS AN awful matter-of-factness about his tone that pulled Skye up short.

'Benoit—'

'I saw her that night,' he said, staring at some distant point in time just over her shoulder. 'I was eight when she left. I'd gone to her room because there had been a horrible storm and I'd woken up from a nightmare. I just didn't realise that I'd gone from one to another.'

Skye's heart lurched in her chest. She knew that there was only one way this story ended but she wasn't sure that she was ready to hear it. But Benoit pressed on.

'Usually her door was locked, which was why I was so surprised, why I entered the room.' Benoit shook his head against the memory, as if wondering at his own actions that night.

'Just like I came into this room just now,' he scoffed angrily. 'She looked almost exactly as you did. A half-packed suitcase on the bed, something

in her hands and a guilty-as-sin look on her face.'
He couldn't stem the tide of acidic bitterness.

'I knew, even as I asked my mother the question, I knew. That she was leaving my father, leaving us. I begged her, *begged* to take me with her. Pleaded and cried like the little child I was. And do you know what the worst thing was? In that moment I would have left Xander behind. I would have abandoned *my brother*,' Benoit spat, hating the memories of that night, how cowardly he had been, how desperately he had begged his mother to take him with her, to love him enough to want to.

'I told her that I hated my father, and that I just wanted to be with her. That I didn't care about Xander. But she kept shaking her head. Kept saying that it was something *she* had to do. That she couldn't take me with her. And then she made me promise not to tell anyone that I'd seen her. Not to say a word to anyone—my father, Xander or Anaïs. Not to cry in case it alerted one of the staff. I was to show no sign that I'd seen her that evening at all.'

Skye's heart was breaking for the little boy who'd not only watched his mother leave, but asked, begged her to take him with her and been refused. She felt fury on his behalf, even knowing that she had nearly done the same thing to him.

'She had no right to ask you to make that promise,' she said to Benoit.

'But I did. And it was the last time I saw her. I went back to my room and waited for the sun to come up, I waited for someone else to make the same discovery I had, but if I'd known that it would have been Xander I…

'I heard him calling for her when he couldn't find her.' He'd watched as Xander tore through the whole house looking for someone who wasn't there any more. He'd watched as Xander's heart had broken. Their father hadn't even looked up from his morning newspaper and coffee, but Xander? He'd cried for two whole weeks.

'I'm so sorry, Benoit.'

'I'm not. It taught me a very valuable lesson. That when it comes down to it, Skye, we *all* become selfish. We all take what it is that we need. So believe me when I say I'm not surprised by your actions. You have the map and you might even be able to find the jewels and do whatever the hell you want with them. But for me? The company is all I have left. And I'm going to make damn sure that I get it.

'Perhaps you think, because of the intimacies we've shared, that I'm someone whose finer feelings can be played upon. Well, don't. Let me be clear—all intimacies are over but the agreement is not. So you'd better still be here tomorrow, because we *will* be announcing our engagement at the party.'

Benoit speared her with a stare, as if to make sure that Skye understood his warning, before throwing something onto the bed beside her case and stalking from the room.

Skye felt as if the earth was shifting beneath her feet. She hurt for the little boy whose mother had abandoned him, who made him make a promise not to cry. A boy who grew into a man who was betrayed again by his girlfriend with his brother. And then by her.

She had done exactly as all those people who had hurt him had—taken what they wanted and left. Or planned to.

As much as she wanted to deny it, she *had* been about to run away.

Because, if she was honest, she'd never thought she'd actually find the map. Yes, she'd desperately hoped and prayed for her mother's sake. But the reality of it? Actually finding it? It had been inconceivable. Because that would mean not only that they might be able to find those jewels, but that she would actually have to marry Benoit.

And in some ways *not* finding the map had made that easier. It had been her get-out clause. It meant that she'd never have to face the fact that she'd marry a man who would never love her. So no, Benoit was wrong. She wasn't running away because of her sisters. She was running from her feelings for him. Because they terrified her. More than anything.

She crossed the room to her bed and picked up the object he had thrown there earlier. It was the ring they had found with the map. The citrine crystal that Benoit had given to Catherine before he'd left England all those years ago glinted in the low lighting of the room.

It had been meant to be her engagement ring Skye now realised as she sank onto the bed, the strange synchronicity touching her heart and breaking it at the same time. Tears gathered at the corners of her eyes and as she leaned back against the headboard she felt paper crumple in her back pocket.

The letter from Benoit's great-great-grandfather. As carefully as she could, she retrieved the aged envelope and with shaking hands began to read.

Dear Ms Soames
Please forgive the assumption of the ad-
dress. I can only assume that Catherine is
right in her faith and belief—as she has been
in so many things—that it will be a female
member of her family who will eventually
unearth what she has hoped to have hidden.
It is a hope we both share.
How does one explain such a thing to

someone who is not yet born, and may not be for some years? It is almost unimaginable. But safe to say that this hope is one born of love. For Catherine, love of her future family, and for me... Love of her.

I have been truly blessed with my wife and family and would not change a single step on the path that led me to them. But Catherine—her strength, her determination, and the joy that shines through those two qualities... She was an incredible person and I feel lucky to have known her.

Ours was an impossible love. We knew it before we acted on it, during and most acutely after we were forced to part ways. Perhaps in the future, society's decrees will be less rigid, marriages will be less confined by duty and class, and love will be less judged. I hope that will be the case, so very much.

For Catherine, the Soames jewels have been a heavy weight to bear. They have brought only cruel, desperate men to her door. Her wish—our wish—is that you find the jewels that are rightfully yours and that they bring you great peace and true love.

You are our hopes and our dreams.

Always,
BC

Noticing the use of the same code that she and her sisters had seen in Catherine's diaries, she traced her fingers over the underlined letters on the page. And the message ran over and over in her mind as she put aside the letter and retrieved the ring. She was humbled and overwhelmed by a message over one hundred and fifty years old that was full of love, compassion and understanding.

And as her heart was torn between what she felt she should do for her sisters and what she wanted to do for Benoit, it broke a little. He was right. Her sisters would be fine. They would *always* be fine because she had done that for them, given them a security she had never felt herself. A small part of her realised then that the instinct to go to them was learned, was ingrained and habitual. She thought of the way Benoit had drawn her out in Costa Rica. Just one day, and over five thousand miles ago.

She slipped the citrine ring onto her engagement finger, a surprised sigh escaping her lips as it fitted perfectly. Her sisters had the map; they had what they needed to take the next step to finding the Soames jewels. It was Benoit who needed her now.

As she shifted back onto the bed, the message from Benoit's letter settled into her heart.

Go with love.

* * *

Skye hadn't seen Benoit all day. She'd slept late, grabbed some lunch and wandered the garden, looking for traces of Benoit's childhood and not quite finding any. Wandering through the beautiful chateau had only made her feel more in the way and uncomfortable as uniformed staff members hustled and bustled about in preparation for what looked to be a spectacular event. So eventually she'd retreated to her rooms and pored over the pages of Catherine's diaries that Summer had typed up and emailed.

Her heart ached for her ancestor, who'd loved a man she would never have been allowed to marry. And here Skye was, about to marry a man who might never love her. To marry a man she was beginning to fear that she really did love. Because the Benoit she had seen in Costa Rica, the incredible man who had drawn her out and shown her what she could be, the man who only hurt here at the chateau, a man convinced that selfishness was at the root of everything, yet he had only given to her...*that* man deserved her love.

Skye cast a glance at the dresses magically procured by Benoit's assistant, and she frowned. They were all perfectly fine, gorgeous even, but not quite...

A knock sounded at the door and her heartbeat picked up.

Benoit.

But as she opened the door to find Anaïs standing there Skye forced down the disappointment and hoped that it didn't show on her face. The little dog yapped a greeting from where he was nestled in her arms and, with an amused eye roll, Anaïs released him to explore Skye's room, dotingly watching as he raced about searching for invisible treats.

'I wanted to see how you were.' Anaïs looked beyond her to the selection of dresses hung in a row across the top of the dresser and scoffed. 'Benoit's assistant is a man with no taste. Business acumen, yes, but absolutely no taste. Trust me, Benoit would *never* have chosen any of these.'

Skye couldn't help but smile at the thought that Anaïs wanted to assure her that her greatnephew had better taste in clothing. But when the older woman's eyes turned back to her, taking her in from head to foot and then narrowing suspiciously, the first stirrings of excitement began to spread in Skye's chest. Because she wanted this evening to be perfect for Benoit. Wanted him to have a fiancée he would not only stand by but be proud of. And she had a feeling that Anaïs wanted that too.

* * *

Pulling at the neck of his shirt, Benoit wondered for the hundredth time how the ballroom had managed to get so hot. For nearly twenty minutes now, his frustration with Skye's absence had grown into a physical thing. He'd barely been able to utter a few civil words to his extended family, resenting each and every one of them for putting him in this situation.

A small rise in volume near the entrance alerted him to a new arrival and he bit back the familiar bitterness that coated his tongue when he finally saw his brother. It took a moment for the image he'd held in his mind and the actual reality of Xander to merge into one. Over the last two years he'd allowed betrayal to morph his brother into a monstrous presence at the back of his mind. But now that Xander was here, greeting members of his family, Benoit was struck dumb. Shocking sentiment clashed against hurt and he didn't know which one would win out. Xander, nearly as tall as his own six foot three inches, bent to greet some of the older generation before casting a glance directly towards him, as if he'd always known where Benoit was in the room.

A set of blue eyes pierced the isolation he had found himself in. Xander's familiar jawline, angular and as determined as his own, clenched as if ready for a confrontation. The murmurs in the room rose once again as the expectation of a showdown increased. Benoit bit off a bitter laugh. As if he'd give them the satisfaction.

The moment his brother made a move in his direction, Benoit purposely turned his back on him, scanning the crowds for any sign of Skye. But he couldn't ignore that he'd felt…not angry, but actually happy to see Xander. For a moment he'd forgotten everything and relief had spread through him at the sight of him. Was it the memories that he'd shared with Skye that had conjured this strange disjointed feeling? He'd admitted to Skye that he would have turned his back on Xander and gone with his mother without a second thought all those years ago, and with it had come the realisation that he'd actually been thankful for Xander's betrayal. Because it had—for the briefest time—overshadowed the years of guilt Benoit had felt. Finally, they were once again equal in their betrayal of each other.

But the ache forming at this thought overshadowed the night. Instead of the guests in the ballroom, he saw trees and branches. Instead of murmured conversations and gentle music, he heard the sounds of boyish laughter. Instead of the rich heady scent of perfume, damp, peaty forest earth filled his nose. Memories of building forts with Xander consumed him, the thoughtless ease and love of their bond stretched through him. The way they had stood together, side by side, with cardboard swords and tea-towel capes, as they faced down imaginary armies. And suddenly what rose up from the last two years wasn't betrayal or bitterness, but loneliness without his brother by his side. The brother he had consulted with each and every business deal, the confidante he had discussed almost every thought and feeling with.

As if pulled up by his own realisation, he was about to turn back to Xander when he noticed each of the guests turning towards the grand circular staircase at the head of the room. Expecting to see his great-aunt, his breath caught in his lungs unexpectedly and his chest seized.

If Anaïs hadn't been holding onto her arm as they rounded the balcony that looked over the huge ballroom, dotted with round tables as if it were a wedding reception, Skye would have stopped in her tracks. A soiree, Anaïs had called it. She was pretty sure Benoit had called it a gathering. This was something *entirely* different.

It reminded her of a ball described in Catherine's diary and, for just a moment, Skye felt the past and present merge. The notion was most definitely helped by the incredible dress that Anaïs had found for her. It had taken her breath away when she'd first seen it. The oyster-coloured silk was floor-length with a small silver waist detail at the front which closed in a ribbon at the back. From the shoulders, two drapes of chiffon veed down to the centre of her waist over the lace detail of the bodice beneath. Skye was thankful for the cap sleeves that left her arms bare in this heat. The lace at her back, exquisitely detailed, crossed her shoulder blades and met at the waist, but it was the skirt that Skye loved most. The silky chiffon fell away from the waist to the floor in thousands of tiny layers, making her look and feel like a princess. The easy glide of it against her skin took her by surprise each time she took a step and it made her feel feminine and sensual in a way she never could have imagined.

As if Anaïs was her fairy godmother and had planned it all, Skye's dress matched the ballroom filled with tables covered in creamy linen tablecloths and pale-coloured dinner sets, the room lit with white candles that hung in wall sconces and from the largest chandeliers she had ever seen.

Everywhere she looked, gold and diamonds twinkled. Music played by a real quartet at one end of the room softened the hum of the quietly spoken conversations rising up from the floor below. Some of the older guests were using fans to cool them from the surprising heat and Skye half expected a footman to be waiting at the top of the stairs that led down to the ballroom to announce her and Anaïs' arrival.

As she scanned the ballroom, looking for Benoit, her eyes snagged on a tall, sandy blond-haired man—the jawline familiar. But while her mind hooked onto the man, her heart knew that this wasn't Benoit and she paused, studying the person who could only be Xander, Benoit's brother.

In an instant Skye wanted to be beside Benoit because she knew that this would be difficult for him. And no matter Benoit's machinations, excuses even, for demanding that she wear his ring…it wasn't about the company. It wasn't about what was rightfully his. Beneath that, Skye had seen the hurt and anger swirling beneath the surface and, no matter how painful his parents' betrayal, Skye knew, *knew*, that the deepest hurt, the deepest guilt, had focused around his feelings for his brother. So she pushed aside the nervousness she felt within her chest and answered Anaïs' shrewd assessing gaze as they stepped towards the top of the staircase with a firm smile. She was ready.

She picked up the skirts of the dress so as not to trip on them or catch them with her heels, casting a look down the stairs to where they were heading. From the corner of her eye, the citrine ring caught the light and sparkled, as if to remind her, *Go with love.*

As they began to descend the staircase, finally her eyes found Benoit and her chest constricted as if she needed his permission to breathe. He was…marvellous. She swore she could feel the power resonating from him. The tuxedo he wore clung to his broad shoulders, dropping to a narrow V just above his waist. The starched white shirt clashed beautifully with the bronze tan of his skin and she couldn't take her eyes off his jaw. Clean shaven, he was even more handsome. As if the beard had softened his impact, it was now painfully clear that he was almost insolently sexy.

Desire shivered across her skin as she refused to drop her gaze, her eyes locked with his with each step that brought her closer and closer to him, with each glide of her silk skirts against her skin, wishing fervently that it was his hands rather than the material of her dress that covered her body.

A blush rose to her cheeks, she could feel the heat of it, not because every single one of the guests had fallen silent at their approach, but because of the sensual magic weaving between them. He stalked towards the bottom of the stairs, the look in his eyes as intense as she felt.

'Thank you for lending Skye to me for the day, but I feel it's time that I returned your fiancée to you.'

Skye registered the few gasps and murmurs

that greeted Anaïs' decree, absently wondering if perhaps this was the first time that Benoit's family had heard the news. But everything paled into insignificance as Anaïs moved Skye's arm from hers to his. It felt…ritualistic—as if she were being presented to him as an offering. As a prize.

Anaïs disappeared and all Skye could see, could think of, could feel was him.

'I didn't think you would still be here.'

'I am. But not because you told me to be, but because I want to be.'

She kept her eyes on his, trying as much as possible to express her meaning, to imprint it upon him so that he would understand the truth behind her words. There was so much she desperately wanted to tell him—her feelings for him, why she had done what she'd done, about her mother—but the guests had now turned to crowd around them, questions on their lips and suspicion in their eyes. So she stayed silent as he led her towards the head table.

As she sat in the chair he pulled out for her, staring down at the sheer number of knives, forks, plates, side plates, first and second course plates, the four glasses—*four*—she tried not to flinch as a uniformed man poured champagne into the flute beside her.

It was only when she felt Benoit stiffen beside her that she realised Xander Chalendar had taken a seat opposite. For a moment the guests around the table seemed to take a collective breath until Anaïs launched into a topic of conversation Skye tried very hard to keep up with.

Noticing that Benoit had barely touched his starter, Skye couldn't help but sneak out a hand beneath the tablecloth, to reach for the clenched fist he held against his thigh. The fierce stretch of skin over knuckles told her how difficult he was finding this and she smoothed her palm over his fist and hoped that it would somehow relax him. She hadn't realised that she was holding her breath until slowly his hand unfurled and his fingers gently threaded through hers. A small smile pulled at her lips and finally she turned her attention back to the delicious food, enjoying the one-handed eating style that they were now both engaged in.

The easy conversation that covered the first and second courses, all the way to dessert, had lulled her into a false sense of security. So it took her a moment to realise that she was being pinned by a stare from Benoit's brother, as if he were waiting for her to make eye contact, demanding it even. When she finally did raise her gaze, she purposely left it open. She wasn't quite sure what she'd expected—suspicion, anger? But instead… truly? She thought she saw some kind of protectiveness in his eyes, recognising it as something

she felt for her sisters. And that kind of protectiveness? It was dangerous and she was immediately on edge.

'So, Miss Soames,' Xander said, as if it weren't
the first thing he'd ever uttered in her direction,
'how long have you known my brother?'

Skye wasn't quite sure what angle he was playing here, because she didn't really know enough
about Xander to assume anything. She knew how
Benoit felt about him and she didn't need the way
he had clenched her hand in his to tell her that he
was suspicious of his brother's motivations. Perhaps Xander wanted to disprove their relationship
to the family so Benoit wouldn't be able to secure the CEO position permanently, perhaps not.
She could hardly ignore the question, but neither
was she going to leave Benoit open to any kind
of suspicion or doubt.

'It feels like years,' she simply replied.

'I'm sure you could forgive us for thinking that
this engagement is oddly fortuitous.'

So he was trying to undermine Benoit. Everything in her rose to his defence and she wouldn't
let this go quietly. She didn't know these people, she didn't care about these people, but she
did know Benoit. He had shown her time and
time again that, despite his hurts, he wanted the
best for his company, his family. He didn't want
to make the same mistakes as his father or his

mother, and not only had he led her to the map, he had shown her a part of herself she had long forgotten.

'I could forgive you for thinking that, but perhaps not for saying it,' she replied.

Xander nodded, accepting the criticism. 'But, with so much at stake, I'm sure that you can understand the family's concern. We would all love to hear how your relationship came into being.'

'Well, you could say that we crashed into each other's lives quite suddenly,' she said, a small smile pulling at her lips. 'And now I couldn't imagine mine without him in it,' she pressed on, surprised at how the sentiment rang true within her.

'I'm presuming the engagement will be short?'

'There's certainly no need to wait,' she fired back, finding strength in the way Anaïs' smile warmed her, while she tried to ignore the brooding anger vibrating from where she touched Benoit.

'I just find it hard to believe that you know each other well enough in such a short space of time,' Xander replied, his eyes flicking between her and Benoit.

Skye let loose a small laugh. 'Ask me anything,' she said, relishing the feeling of power that glowed within her. Because she did, she realised.

She did know Benoit. And, for just a moment, she saw doubt spread across Xander's features.

Holding his gaze now, and refusing to look towards Benoit, she pressed on. 'How he likes his coffee? Black, strong and he doesn't stop until he's had three cups—and please, don't try and talk to him before then, he's impossible.' A small laugh rose from the other guests at the table. 'Benoit likes a very rich red wine, but prefers whisky after dinner. He's proud and hates to admit he's wrong, which, admittedly, is rare but does happen on certain occasions. He has a penchant for crime fiction and autobiographies, likes print books instead of E-readers, and once a year travels to Costa Rica to switch off from the world. No phones, no internet, no neighbours and, more importantly, no contact from the company that every other day of the year he gives one hundred and ten per cent to.'

She saw the moment that surprise entered Xander's gaze, didn't miss the way that Benoit's hand had fallen slightly slack beneath hers and knew that she was about to cross a boundary, but she also knew instinctively that what she was about to say needed to be said. For Benoit and, yes, even for Xander.

'As a child he wanted to be an explorer, but gave it up for family duty. He still misses the forts that he once built with you in the forest here and, although he probably wouldn't admit to it on pain of death, he bitterly regrets the distance between both of you now. Something that may be undermined by your rather uncouth assertions that my relationship with him is built on nothing more than a desire to control the family company.'

Silence met her declaration until Anaïs shifted beside her, a sheen of tears glistening in the older woman's gaze.

'You love him,' she stated rather than asked. 'Why?'

'Because he saw me when I couldn't yet see myself,' she answered simply and honestly while her heartbeat raged within her chest. 'Now, if you'll excuse me, I think I'll retire for the night.'

CHAPTER ELEVEN

Nearly an hour later and fury still roiled within Benoit's chest. Just when he had been softening towards his brother, Xander had gone on the attack. He cursed as he stalked back to his room.

For the first time he'd actually wanted to strike his brother. Camilla's betrayal hadn't even affected him like this. The only thing that had prevented him from launching across the table at Xander had been Skye. Her words. Her declaration.

And that had floored him. She'd left not only him but the entire table in shocked silence as she'd regally retreated from the ballroom. But, once the shock had faded, the fury he felt towards his brother was nothing.

You love him.

Even Anaïs had been able to see it. Clear as day. And Benoit knew that Skye wasn't that good a liar.

She had shown her vulnerability. And he knew

himself. He would take it and use it. His selfishness meant he would bend her to his will. His mind showed a kaleidoscope of his misdeeds, countless broken hearts, his brother... Even before, when he'd been fighting his selfish nature, he could hardly pretend that he had offered Camilla a proper relationship. He'd not been there at all, working all hours for his company, selfish even then. And he would ruin Skye. He simply couldn't let that happen.

The betrayal this time was not Xander's—it never had been. It had been his own.

He pulled up in front of his bedroom door, knowing that she would be there, needing to steady himself. To push down the roiling emotions that were making him nauseous. It was all her fault.

He found her perched on the end of his bed, waiting for him. The smooth silks of her cream dress presented her as the perfect package. But Benoit knew there was no such thing as perfect.

'I've arranged for the jet to take you anywhere you want to go,' he announced, his tone bland and completely emotionless.

'And why would I want to go anywhere?' Her tone matched his and it infuriated him.

'Because our deal is done,' he growled, unable to keep the leash on his feelings he'd been so proud of only moments ago.

'What do you mean? We aren't married, the company—'

'The company is a family matter and you are not family.'

He could see that his words had struck home and hard, exactly as intended, but it didn't make the slash of guilt slicing into his heart any easier to bear. But bear it he would, because he was going to have earned it by the end of this night.

'So they're just going to change their minds?' she asked, suspicion shining up from the dark depths of her brown eyes.

'I'm done with being manipulated from beyond the grave by my own ancestors. Aren't you?'

'I don't have much choice,' Skye said, this time something unreadable passing across her gaze. He ignored it, he had to focus. 'I—'

'You have what you need. You have the map, so you can go.'

'What if I want to stay? You might not be ready to hear it, but will you let me show you?' she asked. He knew what she wanted—wanted it himself—but he couldn't let her touch him. He knew that if she did that he'd be lost. And he'd already lost too damn much.

'I said that this part of our relationship was at an end.'

'I know what you said, and I understand why you said it—' sympathy and desire warring in her eyes. 'You were right when you accused me of running away, but not about the reason why,' she said, standing up and stepping towards him. 'And I think that you are also hiding from the very same thing, trying to control it, by denying this.'

She pressed a kiss against his lips—lips he refused to move, no matter how every single cell in his body rioted with the need to take her in his arms.

'Because this is terrifying,' she said, pressing yet another kiss against his lips, her hand coming up to claim his clean-shaven jaw. 'Because it makes us both feel out of control,' she stated, pressing her chest against his, firing need and desire deep within him. He feared that the internal tremors shaking him would be seen, the fierce battle between his desire for her and his need to reject what Skye was saying, reject what she was feeling, raging in his chest.

The softness of her lips met the firm, immovable line of his own. 'But, with you, I find that I like it. I want it. And I want you. Because I...'

And then it was too much. He had to stop her before she said it again, before she could claim him as hers, as she had done at the dinner. Because he didn't think he could survive it. He didn't think he'd be able to let her go.

His lips opened to hers, cutting her off mid-sentence and, as if he'd opened the floodgates, she poured into him, his mouth, his lungs, his veins, all he could sense was her. It blocked out all thought, all of the chaos in an instant; all he knew was her touch, her scent...*her*.

His hand flew to the back of her neck, cradling her head at an angle where he could feast upon her. His fingers tightened in the silken strands of her hair as she moaned her desire into his mouth. Her hands went to his chest, pulling, pushing, grasping him to her as he was pulling her to him. Every thrust of her tongue met the demands of his, as if suddenly all the power they both contained was coming together in a clash of thunder and lightning.

It wasn't enough. This kiss, this raw, feral thing within him, wasn't easing, wasn't satiated; it demanded more—*he* needed more. But more was absolutely impossible. He would ruin them both.

He broke the kiss and turned away, but not before he'd seen the shock and hurt across her painfully expressive eyes. It was something he would never forget for the rest of his life.

'Repeating past mistakes, Skye? Making a gift of yourself? Thanking me for the map?'

She reared back as if she had been slapped. 'Don't say that. Don't do that.'

But he couldn't stop. The words were like ash on his tongue, the pain in her eyes burning his heart, but it was the only way he could make sure that he didn't destroy her completely.

'Then don't belittle yourself by thinking that one night and one sexual awakening means you should beg to be with me.'

He watched her clench her jaw against the numerous terms of abuse she could throw at him, none more colourful or worse than what he was throwing at himself. But still she didn't move. His gut twisted in a knot he thought would never come undone as he forced the words he knew would hurt the most to his lips.

'It's time for you to leave, Skye. I don't need you any more.'

I don't need you any more.

Three weeks, three days ago even, that would have scarred her, scraped at deep hurts that she'd hidden from herself for years. It would have devastated her, would definitely have her running for the hills, no doubt as Benoit intended.

Oh, it hurt. Very much. But not enough to make her leave. Because in the last few days he had opened a door within her. A door that should have been opened years ago. He had made her really look at herself. At what *she* wanted from life. Now and in the future. It wasn't the dependence of her sisters, or approval from her father and his wife. It wasn't the fairy-soft wistfulness of her mother's acceptance either. But neither was it Benoit's money, his Costa Rican holiday home or the vaguely intimidating wealth she saw here in France. It was what she saw in his eyes when he looked at her every time she embraced who she was a bit more. It was the encouragement, the pleasure she saw—*knew*—he got from her being even more of herself each and every day.

No one had ever cared for her like that before. And it was precisely that sense of empowerment that allowed her to see through the walls that Benoit had built up around his heart, causing her to say, 'That's a lie.'

'Really, Skye, all this is making you look a little desperate.'

'And you scared,' she replied quickly before his verbal strike could draw blood. 'Beneath it all, you're just a coward. Because it's not me, Camilla or even Xander that you don't trust. It's yourself. That's why you disappear off to Costa Rica with no access to the outside world. Why you jump from impossibly tall waterfalls. You're seeing if you can trust yourself to be completely self-sufficient, because you're scared of depending on or needing someone again.'

'Don't you dare bring her into this,' he warned, his body physically trembling from the effort it was taking to hold himself in check. No matter. It was all or nothing—Skye knew that the moment she'd told his family that she loved him.

'Benoit, for so long the thing you've clung to from the night your mother ran away is your *almost* betrayal of Xander. You hold it to you as if it's evidence that you're a terrible person. But you were just a child who wanted to stay with his mother, no matter what. Because it was something you could control, the guilt you felt. Rather than what you couldn't—the fact that your mother left. And you've spent so long focusing on that guilt that when Xander betrayed you, *that* became your sole focus.'

'You don't know what you're talking about.'

'You think I don't know how painful it is to be abandoned by a parent and not just once, but again and again? My father chose his new family over me every chance he got. So yes, I do know what I'm talking about.'

She wanted him to see. Not for herself. She had very little hope now that he would relent, that he would keep her with him. But she did want him to see what was shaping the decision he was making. If only to stop him from doing the same in the future.

When she looked into his eyes for a moment she saw unfathomable hurt swirling dark inky streaks into his crystal-blue eyes. Until it passed and she saw…nothing. Complete absence.

'Are you so desperate to forge a connection between us that you will dig out our deepest hurts to compare them? *Mon Dieu*, Skye, how much more do I have to hurt you before you'll just leave?'

She knew then that she'd lost him. His eyes were dark, his jaw determined. Determined to refuse to see the truth of her words.

'Keep the ring,' he said to her. 'It was always meant for a Soames.'

With her heart trembling in her breast, she asked, 'Do you know why Catherine gave the ring back to Benoit? Despite the fact that she loved him then and always would?'

'Because she knew she had to set him free.'

With that he left and took Skye's heart with him.

Benoit didn't care that the tree stump he sat on was damp and it was seeping into his trousers as he took another swing of whisky from the bottle. It had been three days since Skye had left and it had rained almost constantly since then, as if the heavens were punishing him.

An ache had opened up in his chest the moment she'd accused him of covering over the hurt from his mother's abandonment with guilt, with misdirection, with almost everything other than the realisation of the damage his mother had done that night. It was as if all the years of suppressing it had magnified it, compounded it, and Skye had unlocked a door and it was escaping on one long scream of pain that seemed unending and only grew louder and louder with each passing hour.

All this time he'd been focusing on the pain of betrayal by others, by Camilla and his brother, even his own act of betrayal, and he'd not once thought about the little boy who had promised not to cry. Not to tell anyone. Had he kept that promise all these years? Was he still keeping that promise?

He looked up at the remnants of a fort long ago forgotten by two boys and wondered what on earth he was supposed to do now. His musings were cut short when he heard the soft crunch of wet twigs and he knew, without even having to turn, that Xander had found him.

'Leave,' Benoit said from behind closed eyes. 'Leave now or you'll regret it. It's not an empty threat this time.'

'I'm not going anywhere. I'm not letting you push me away. Not like last time.'

'Are you kidding me? You slept with Camilla! You betrayed me,' he shouted, desperately clinging to a source of anger that pointed outward rather than in. Because, honestly, he feared that this time he'd break.

'Camilla was a monumental mistake. I knew that even before I did it, but she was relentless,' Xander said, sitting opposite him on a fallen tree. 'And I was weak…' The words fell from his lips as if in defeat. 'You were so much to live up to, big brother. *Too* much. For almost my entire life you did everything for me. Looked after me, guided me. Protected me,' he said, the words almost painful for Benoit to hear. Because they were true. Benoit had done almost everything and anything he could, attempting to make up for his unknown betrayal.

'When I said it had to stop she told me she was pregnant.'

'What?' Benoit was yanked out of his introspection with an almost electric shock. Pins and needles dragged along his skin. *They had a child?*

'That's why I married her.'

Confusion spread through Benoit, short-circuiting his brain.

'But she lied. It was *all* a lie,' Xander said bitterly. 'She only wanted to be married to the CEO of Chalendar Enterprises and when I told her that it would never be me she left.'

'What do you mean?'

'I came here to tell you that I'm leaving the company,' Xander said, swiping a hand over his face, that now revealed an incredible amount of exhaustion. But, instead of sympathy, Benoit felt anger.

'Then what the hell was all that about the other night? Interrogating Skye about her feelings for me.'

He was surprised to find the ghost of a smile playing at the edges of his brother's mouth.

'At first I thought your relationship was just a marriage of convenience. And I wanted to ruin it because I didn't want you repeating the same mistakes our father made.' Benoit was pierced by his brother's fierce gaze. 'I didn't want you to sacrifice everything for this damn family company. I wanted to free you from it. Benoit, you've given everything and more for it, but it will never give you what you need and it will never make up for what we lost. And when I realised that she loves you—well, I didn't think you'd be stupid enough to push her away too.'

Benoit felt sick, a nausea that mounted as he scanned over the events of the past. Xander and Camilla, her evil machinations that had severed their connections more easily than his pleas to his mother had done. Meeting Skye, and the times that they had shared, the hurt in her eyes as he had thrown the ring on the bed, the shock on her face as he'd turned to leave. Had he really thought that becoming CEO was worth all she had to offer him?

Finally, he looked at his brother and deeply regretted the years they'd been apart, regretted how he'd let the hurt and betrayal overwhelm him to the point where he'd lost his closest friend. And he'd worn that loneliness around him like a cloak, as if that would protect him from what was worse…love. And the deepest, greatest pain that love could bring.

A pent-up breath escaped his lungs. 'I had no idea about Camilla. I can't even begin to imagine…lying about pregnancy like that. It's unspeakable.' He watched as Xander shrugged it off, but could only imagine the pain that his brother must have felt when he'd realised how Camilla had lied. 'For so long,' Benoit said, finally ready to admit his failing, 'it was easier to blame you, to be furious with you, than to admit the truth.'

'What truth?'

'The guilt I felt because of our mother. For allowing her to leave that night. I saw her. I knew what she was doing. I…begged to go with her. I would have left you,' he admitted, shaking his head and unable to look his brother in the eye.

'And, had it been me, I might have done the same,' he heard his brother say as he felt his hand on his shoulder. 'Benoit, our parents made their own decisions and were solely responsible for them. I think that we've spent too long focused on the past and not enough focused on the future. Because you need to get your head on straight if you're going to go after the woman you so clearly love.'

Benoit shook his head. 'I can't…' He gritted

his teeth until his jaw ached. Everything ached. 'It's too much.'

Xander reached for the bottle hanging loosely in Benoit's hands and took a long mouthful. 'I'm surprised you haven't figured it out yet,' his brother said. Benoit threw a frown his way in query. 'That the pain of losing someone is absolutely *nothing* compared to hurting someone you love.'

Skye looked out across the stubble of the harvested fields behind the little cottage that Anaïs had taken her to, letting out a jagged breath that caught on the edges of the pain that had speared her chest since leaving Benoit.

She'd done as he'd requested, collected her things and packed a bag—but, as her hand had reached for the door knob, she'd realised that she didn't want to go back to England to see her sisters.

Not until she'd worked out her true feelings. Because there had been a horrible kernel of truth to what Benoit had said that night. So she'd tracked down Anaïs, who had somehow understood the garbled words Skye had managed to form around the lump in her throat and the ache in her chest. The older woman had simply smiled, patted her hand and led her to a car. Skye smiled through the hurt at the memory of Anaïs dismissing her driver, and soon understood the panic in the chauffeur's eyes as she recalled the dangerous driving that had brought the two women to this gorgeous little country cottage.

Anaïs had ensured that the cottage was stocked with enough food and supplies for as long as Skye needed it, and left only once Skye had assured her that she would be okay. It was a lie. She knew it. Anaïs knew it. But they both tacitly agreed to believe it for the moment.

The cottage was surrounded by fields which, aside from the beautiful garden, were the only thing to be seen for miles around. Which was a good thing, because Skye had done nothing but cry for the first two days. She cried for herself, for Benoit, for what they might have had.

She hadn't answered her sisters' calls, texts or emails. How ironic it was that they had begun to worry about her *now*. She'd called each of them two days ago, explaining a little about what had happened, a little of what she had managed to work through and a lot about how much she loved them, saying that she just needed some time and space. She'd promised to be in touch soon.

All the while, Benoit's words rang like accusations in her mind and she knew that he was right. That she had to let her sisters go, to stop focusing on them and live her life. She wondered now at the person who had found her strength with him in Costa Rica. The taste of it had been addictive and truly life-enhancing. But she knew that she needed to find that within herself, rather than borrowing it from Benoit. And that would take time.

When the sun dipped below the horizon Skye had taken to lighting the wood-burner in the small living room of the cottage. She knew it was a luxury—the summer's warmth was still enough to keep the cool nights mild—but each night she looked for the heat from the flames to draw out the cold ache she felt in her heart.

She had been reading the journals that Summer had typed up. This morning a new section had appeared in her inbox, a note reassuring her that her sisters loved her and were there if she needed them. And Skye was beginning to wonder if it might be about time for her to lean on them for a change. It wasn't easy and it wouldn't seem natural, but it was right.

At first, she'd thought she'd find it painful to read about Catherine and her Benoit. And it was. She'd cried with Catherine over the loss of Benoit Chalendar. At how, once Catherine's father had discovered the affair, he'd forced her to let him go. Benoit's family had been no way near a match for a peer of the realm. Skye had found some kind of solidarity with Catherine's feelings of hurt and anguish as they'd echoed her own.

And felt the determination ring within her own breast as Catherine had forged a way forward, to the Middle East with her uncle, determined to put the pain behind her. The Middle East, where Star was now searching for the second part of the puzzle—the key to the hidden room.

And yesterday she'd called her mother. Skye knew instinctively that she wasn't yet ready to confront her feelings about her father, the pain was too raw. But her mother…they needed to talk. Skye hated that this was over the phone, but the need to speak to her had become urgent, an almost physical need, so that when her mother asked her if she was okay, the simple relief had her crying nonsensically down the phone for about fifteen minutes, while her beautiful, kind, generous mother poured equally nonsensical words of comfort and love back until Skye's sobs subsided.

Even now, a lump formed in her throat, thinking of the pure unconditional love of that moment and the sadness not only of what she had missed out on as a child by trying to fit in halfway with her father and halfway with her mother, which had made her feel like an outsider in both homes, but of what she was surely to miss out on in the future, even if they did manage to find the jewels.

Mariam Soames had offered to get on a plane and they had both laughed, knowing that neither had the money and that Mariam wasn't well enough to go anywhere. So instead her mother had promised Skye that she had a cup of camomile tea, a large blanket, a comfy chair and was ready for her to start at the very beginning.

And although Skye's story had started at Elias Soames' funeral, jumped to Costa Rica and back to her own childhood, touched on the overheard conversation between her father and his wife, about Skye's wildness and about her university education, moved on to Benoit and Anaïs, Catherine and her Benoit, and finished at Skye's little hideout in France, Mariam Soames was there for every single minute of it, offering comfort, kindness, understanding and sympathy. Not once did she ask why Skye hadn't told her any of this before, or chastise her for secrets and hurts kept hidden. Until Skye had worked herself up to the worst hurt, the worst confession—that she'd been keeping her mother at a distance because she'd been ashamed of her.

The second of silence from her mother was the longest moment of her entire life.

'My love, in my eyes it is the responsibility of a child to form their identity against that of their parents. I did it with Elias. And you did it with me. It doesn't make me shameful, or you boring.'

'And Elias?' Skye half joked.

'Well, he was always a nasty piece of work,'

replied her mother sadly. 'Skye, I know that my…
lifestyle was difficult on you. Difficult for our
neighbours and your teachers and the parents of
your friends. I am sorry for that—I'm not apologising for my choices, because I stand by every
one of them. But I am sorry for the hurt and confusion it caused you. I don't like speaking for
your father, because it has been a very long time
since I knew him well enough to do so, but…his
character is simply not as strong as yours, mine,
and most especially his wife's. He does love you,
Skye. He was just never that in touch with his
emotions to be able to show it so well.'

Skye let that sink in. Truly sink in to a depth
that she hoped might begin to bring acceptance.
They'd spoken some more and Skye had promised to call in a few days when she knew what her
plans would be. It hadn't been an easy conversation and there would be harder times ahead, especially with her father, but, whatever happened
with the jewels—if she and her sisters did somehow manage to find them, and sell the estate to
help pay for her mother's medical bills—Skye
knew that the healing that had come from their
conversation would sustain her throughout her
life.

Just before hanging up, her mother had asked
why she hadn't told Benoit the truth about what
she would use the money for if they found the

jewels. There was no censure in her mother's voice, but Skye had felt it all the same. She'd told herself one hundred excuses since that moment, all of which had been both simultaneously true and false. That at first she hadn't trusted him and then later he hadn't trusted her was true... but not reason enough.

And while she had intended to tell him the night of the ball...in some ways it had been a relief not to. Because, deep down, she knew that revealing this would make her the most vulnerable she'd ever been. How he responded to that could break her into a million pieces.

'And it could also give you the support you would need.'

'Mum, please don't talk like that.'

'I don't mean about me. Well, not *just* about me. You were doing yourself a disservice by not letting him be there for you, by not letting him be the man you believe he is.'

'But what if he's not, Mum?'

'I don't see how that's possible,' Mariam said confidently. 'You wouldn't have fallen in love with him if he wasn't.'

And that was it. As if it were that simple. The thought of the raw vulnerability of telling him about Mariam made Skye's heart quiver in her chest. But the hope that her mother had given her, the fact that she *did* know Benoit, *did* believe him to be good at heart soothed some of her fears and for the first time since leaving the chateau she considered the possibility of seeing him again.

Whether they found the jewels or not, whether they were able to do so in time for her mum's treatment, whether she would actually go to university or not, Skye knew that there were some big changes she wanted to make in her life. And they wouldn't cost a thing.

She would not be torn any more by what people expected or wanted from her. She would work hard to listen to herself, to find what it was she wanted to do or be. And, although everything screamed within her that the answer to that was inextricably linked to Benoit Chalendar, she knew that was something she had no control over.

Skye pulled the shawl around her shoulders as the first bite of the evening's chill edged into the air. She turned to head back into the cottage but pulled up short when she saw the figure standing in front of the back door, believing that she was simply imagining it.

For a second, her eyes drank in the sight of Benoit, as if starved by the lack of it in her life. She thought then that it was one of the most marvellous sights she'd ever seen. Until she looked closer and saw the dark hollows beneath his eyes, the shade of stubble across his jaw.

He took a step towards her and Skye stepped

back to keep the distance between them. Because she wasn't sure that she would be able to resist the desperate longing to reach out to him, to touch him, pull him to her.

'What do you want?' she asked instead.

'I would like, very much, for you to hear me out, if you will?'

She nodded, because it was all she could do, her entire body and brain short-circuited by his presence. He gestured towards the old wooden bench beside the rosebush at the edge of the garden and, on stiff legs, she made her way to it. Finally, he sat beside her, leaning his elbows against his knees and looking out across the same field that she had previously been studying.

'Xander and I went to the shareholders' meeting two days ago,' Benoit started to explain, knowing that it was perhaps the wrong place, but the only place he could begin. 'We told them that they could enforce the by-law if they wanted, but that they didn't have to. It was their choice and both Xander and I were willing to abide by that choice. I told them that I should be CEO of Chalendar Enterprises not because I was married, but because I am damn good at it and I want it.' He tried to ignore the way she stiffened beside him and pressed on, hoping that she'd see the truth of his words. 'I do, but not badly enough to bind a kind, loving, amazing woman to me for the sake of it. So I need you to know that I would walk away if needed. Either way, Xander is stepping down from the company and…' he let out a small surprised laugh of his own '…we're going into business together,' he finished, smiling ruefully. If anything good had come out of the awfulness of the last few days it was that he had started to forge the kind of relationship he'd always wanted with his brother, not based on perceived guilt or debt but an honest one. It was interesting and a little like walking through a minefield, but they were getting there.

'I need you to know that before I tell you what I came here to say,' he said, still staring out at the fields as dusk began to draw over them. He clung to that view, a view he'd never seen before but would remember for the rest of his life. 'That you were right. I have spent years throwing distraction after distraction at the hurt my mother caused by leaving. It was so much easier to do that, to blame myself or others, than to recognise that hurt. Which was why I thought it was easier to push others away before they could inflict more of that hurt. But, as someone disturbingly wise pointed out, that pain was nothing compared to what I felt when I hurt you.'

He couldn't look at her. Not yet. He needed

to finish what he'd come here to say, otherwise he'd lose it.

'I will never be able to apologise for...' He could barely force the words out through the terrible memory of the words he'd used against her that day. 'What I said was unforgivable. I belittled the time we spent together and I undermined you and everything that is powerful, glorious and incredible about you. Skye, please know that I will bear the scars of that hurt, that pain I caused you, on my heart for the rest of my life,' he promised, for the first time in his life not caring that his vision had become blurred from the threat of tears.

'You were also right when you said I was a coward. Even when I was hurting you, saying cruel things to push you away. I thought I was doing it to protect you from me, but I was wrong. It was because I was scared of the strength of my own feelings for you. You fought against me and *for* me. I was...scared because I've never been as happy as I was in Costa Rica with you, because I love you.'

Finally, he turned to look at her and his heart nearly broke in two when he saw the tears gathered in her eyes. 'I love you,' he said again. He might even have said it another time before she put her fingers to his lips and his heart dropped. He reached for her hands as if to hold her to him, but she pulled back and looked out at the same view he had just been desperately clinging to.

'Thank you,' she said, tucking her hand back under her thigh. 'I...thank you for apologising for what you said that night.'

He felt nauseous all of a sudden, only now realising that he might have truly lost all hope.

Skye hadn't missed the way that he had blanched before she had turned her attention to the horizon. But she'd had to turn away or she would never be able to say what she needed to. Shaking her head, blind to the beauty of the setting sun, she just marvelled.

'How can it only have been eight days?' she whispered, feeling the weight of his eyes on her face, neck, hair. 'In Costa Rica you made me see things about myself that I'd not even thought were possible. You helped me... No, you *made* me confront things about myself that I'd never told anyone. You were also right. I think, because of the way I grew up, I would make myself into what I thought people wanted from me so that they would...' she breathed around the sob welling in her chest '...so that they would keep me.' A tear dropped from where it had grown thick and round at the corner of her eye. She hastily swept it away.

'But you?' she said, a laugh in her voice this time. 'You didn't want me in the first place.'

'Skye—'

She couldn't help but laugh properly now. A sense of joy was building in her.

I love you. I love you. I love you.

She'd remember his words for the rest of her life.

'It's okay. Who would want a complete stranger literally crashing their one and only holiday, where they got to go off and be all—'

'Mancenary?'

'Exactly!' she said, her eyes turning to him, flashing bright with fun and love and everything in between. For the first time she saw a glint of hope shining amongst the icy shards of his blue eyes like a diamond. 'You must have thought me completely crazy, getting drunk and talking about missing jewels and secret passageways.'

'Never,' he said so sincerely she knew he was joking.

'But Benoit,' she said, finally looking at him, all the love she felt for him rising up and pouring out of her, knowing that she was safe, that her love was safe because she could see it shining in him. 'Who knew that, beneath all that mansplaining,' she said, reaching up to cup his jaw, running her thumb against the stubble he'd allowed to grow since the night of the ball, relishing the way he captured her hand in his, holding her to him, 'and all those terse monosyllabic replies, was the only man I would ever truly love?'

He took her hands in his then, his eyes open and expressing every single thing he felt. Pain, guilt, but also hope and love.

'I'm so sorry that I caused you such pain.'

'The pain was always there, you just exposed it to sunlight, allowing it to heal. Allowing me to really embrace my love for you without giving myself away. I *do* love you because you allowed me to have that control in my life, you showed me that I can be strong and powerful and allow others the freedom to love me for who I am and not what I can be for them.'

Skye took a deep breath, her heart full with happiness, sadness, a little bit of grief and a whole lot of love. 'But I also need to talk to you about something before I can say anything else. Because I'm going to need you to love me through this.'

He frowned and took her hand as if sensing the gravity of it. Slowly and with halting words, Skye explained how her mother had been diagnosed with stage three cancer and how they had just missed out on the most successful treatment the NHS had to offer because of where they lived. He held her hand as the tears fell and Skye confessed that the sisters only wanted the diamonds so that they could sell the estate and pay for Mariam's treatment, he held her—shaking in his arms—as she revealed that she'd been scared of telling him because if he did this, if he supported her, loved her through this then she wasn't sure that she would ever be able to let him go.

He told her that she'd never have to let him go as he wiped the tears from her cheeks. He promised her that together they would find either the treatment or the jewels, whatever it took to keep Mariam healthy for as long as possible, as he pressed gentle kisses to her forehead, eyelids, cheeks and mouth. He took her hand and placed it over his heart and told her that it belonged not just to her, now and always, but to her family, her sisters and mother, and that she would never face a hardship alone ever again.

'Then I will marry you tomorrow, or any other day before your birthday if that's what you want,' Skye promised him, feeling as if she were soaring into clouds with the love that she felt within and around her.

Benoit gazed at her, moving so slowly that she almost hauled him to her—and, as if realising that, a smile curved the corner of his lip upwards and she'd never seen him look so devastating as he was in that moment.

'You are so beautiful,' he said, placing a kiss on her cheek. 'So perfect,' he said, kissing her neck.

'So incredible,' he said, his lips gently pressing against hers. 'I have done nothing to deserve you,' he said. 'But I promise to spend the rest of my life trying to do so.'

He kissed her then, a slow building, powerful roll of lips and tongues and heat and love that threatened to take her breath away. They stayed there, kissing like teenagers until the moon came out and the stars twinkled as if laughing with them.

'We should go in,' Skye said reluctantly.

As if suddenly realising that inside there were many more options, like beds, and sofas, Benoit's eyes brightened. 'We should! We definitely should. But,' he said, his eyes growing serious, 'before we do… I won't be marrying you tomorrow.'

Skye pulled up short in confusion as his words seemed to contradict each other.

'I do want to marry you, more than anything I've ever wanted before. But I also want you to know that it's not because of any possible connection to the company. So, Skye Soames, would you do me the honour of waiting until a year from today to marry me on my thirty-third birthday?'

She laughed, shock and a happy sort of surprise soaring in her breast. To know that, no matter what happened with the company, this was his gift to her. To know that he truly did love her, no matter what.

'A year?' she asked.

'Yes.'

'Well, I suppose that will give you plenty of time.'

'Time for what?'

'For you to teach me how to ride a motorbike.'

EPILOGUE

THREE HUNDRED AND sixty-five days later and Skye was standing in front of a floor-length antique gold mirror in the most beautiful wedding dress she'd ever seen. Delicate lace detail smoothed over silk that draped perfectly over and around her incredibly large baby bump, making her smile even more.

'Oh, Skye,' her mum cried from behind her, tears of joy glistening in her eyes. 'I never thought…' Skye watched as Mariam Soames pressed her lips together, holding back the words as Star reached for her mother's hands and Summer placed her head on Mariam's shoulder.

All four women knew the end of that sentence. Knew how close they'd come to not having this moment. So much had happened in the last year, highs, lows, fraught battles and hard-won victories, each one bringing them to a love and happiness that they never could have expected. Skye turned and was instantly wrapped in the loving embrace of the women she shared her life with.

'If you start crying...' Star warned through her own tears.

'It will ruin your eyeliner and that took me almost ten minutes to get right,' finished Summer, with the same sheen of tears as her sister and mother.

'You know weddings are supposed to be happy, right?' Skye chided. 'And that you're not supposed to cry until the end?'

'But it's—'

'So *romantic*,' Skye, Summer and Mariam Soames finished for Star, before they all descended into gentle giggles.

There was a knock on the door and Xander, Benoit's best man, called out the time, alerting the girls to the fact that the ceremony was to start shortly. Skye ushered them all from the room with a smile, just wanting a moment to herself. With promises that she'd be down in a minute, she turned back to the mirror and took in the glow in her cheeks, the shine to her hair—a nice boon from her pregnancy—and the glint of the citrine ring on her finger the most magical of all. In some ways, it was even more special than the diamond necklace that hung from her neck, dropping low into the V of the bodice of her wedding dress. One third of the Soames jewels, the other two with her sisters, making it feel—as it always had done—as if some things were meant to be.

Life had changed so much in the last year. The moment Skye had returned to England with Benoit and been reunited with her sisters, to hear the accounts of their own fantastic journeys, her mother had been rushed into treatments that had dramatically changed everything. It had not been easy and, a year on, the only thing they knew the future held for certain was hope. And that wouldn't have been possible without Catherine Soames.

During that time, Skye had grown in confidence, had let go of the responsibilities she had placed upon herself and started to embrace her inner thrill-seeker, all of which had been down to her future husband—even if he did regret showing her how to ride a motorbike. She had fallen in love with the Dordogne and her French was improving every day, which was invaluable as they now split their time between England and France. But the love, the certainty and security she had found with Benoit was something she marvelled at the most, never imagining how powerful a thing it was to love and be loved without measure.

And, no matter how long she lived, she would never forget that she wouldn't have met Benoit without the Soames jewels. Wouldn't have rushed headlong into an adventure that—she now knew—had only just begun when she slipped into an unlocked car. And she hadn't been the only one, as Star's part in finding the Soames' jewels had been just as magical and exciting as her own, but that was a story for another time.

Downstairs, more than two hundred guests were taking their seats on the white chairs with large white bows on the beautiful green lawn in front of the wildflower arbour beneath which she would declare her love for Benoit. She bit down on her bottom lip when she thought on the fact that her father wasn't amongst them. It didn't hurt as much as it would have a year ago, but she wouldn't deny herself the moment to honour that feeling, before letting it go.

Frowning, she felt something draw her to the window and she had learned in the last year to pay attention to her instincts. With a smile already pulling at her lips, she pulled the curtain across her body to cover her dress, conscious of the superstition about wedding gowns and thankful that she had. Down on the grassy bank, as people made their way towards their seats, stood Benoit, staring up as if they'd arranged to meet like this.

He looked at her with wonder, as if he'd never seen anything more beautiful than her, as if he'd never stop looking at her. She watched as he covered his heart with his hand and then pressed it to his mouth. She would swear until her last day that she felt his lips against hers in that moment. But, in truth, they didn't need words, they didn't need touches, or kisses—they were, of course, welcome and wonderful—but unnecessary because she felt more than his kiss. She felt his soul entwine with hers, making her more than just herself, making them greater together. Skye no longer feared being herself, no longer feared past hurts or future pains because, whatever storm would come, they would survive it.

Because they would always *go with love*.

* * * * *

Blown away by
Terms of Their Costa Rican Temptation?
Look out for the next instalment in
The Diamond Inheritance trilogy

Why not also explore these other stories
by Pippa Roscoe?

Virgin Princess's Marriage Debt
Demanding His Billion-Dollar Heir
Taming the Big Bad Billionaire
Rumours Behind the Greek's Wedding
Playing the Billionaire's Game

All available now!